D0523507

NEW SKIN FOR THE
OLD CEREMONY

UNCORRECTED PROOF
NOT FOR QUOTATION OR RESALE

UNCORRECTED PROOF – NOT FOR QUOTATION OR RESALE

Published by 404 Ink
www.404Ink.com
@404Ink

All rights reserved © Arun Sood, 2022.

The right of Arun Sood to be identified as the Author of this Work has been asserted by him in accordance with the Copyright, Designs and Patent Act 1988.

No part of this publication may be reproduced, distributed, or transmitted, in any form or by any means, electronic, mechanical, photocopying, recording, or otherwise, without first obtaining the written permission of the copyright owner, except for the use of brief quotations in reviews.

This is a work of fiction. Names, characters, business, events and incidents are the products of the author's imagination. Any resemblance to actual persons, living or dead, or actual events is purely coincidental

Editing: Craig Hillsley
Typesetting: Laura Jones
Cover design: Rafaela Romaya
Co-founders and publishers of 404 Ink:
Heather McDaid & Laura Jones

ISBN: 9781912489534
ebook: 9781912489541

Printed and bound in Great Britain by Clays Ltd, Elcograf S.p.A.

404 Ink acknowledges and is thankful for support from Creative Scotland in the publication of this title.

LOTTERY FUNDED

New Skin for the Old Ceremony

A KIRTAN

ARUN SOOD

THE

PROLOGUE

A ROADSIDE SOUTH OF OLD MANALI

The four of them sat smoking charas on a roadside some-where south of Old Manali. Liam thumbed through a pam-phlet he picked up in McLeod Ganj. It was called *The Universe Unfolds Itself*. He read from it softly.

—When stars die, particles formed within them are flung out into space. The stardust gets incorporated into new stars, planets, moons, and meteorites. Matter arises from death.

Liam looked skywards. Bobby broke his silence.

—Aye, and people think reincarnation is stupid?

Viddy and Raj stretched their backs, *Virabhadrasana 1*, Warrior Pose.

The mountain ridge dimmed to a turquoise silhouette. The bikes glowed orange as the sun slipped away.

THE

KIRTANKARA

RAJEEV SABHARWAL (RAJ)

A silent sterility fell over the dusking second bedroom of Raj and Ibti's third-floor Deptford apartment. Grey streaks of late London light added colour to porcelain walls, provoking an undefined melancholy over the failings of the powder spray paint can Raj was wielding. He was trying to decorate what had recently been dubbed "the baby room", and previously called "the art studio". But for every snowy ejaculation of glow-in-the-dark paint, the stencil frame of stars lifted to reveal his creations flake and flounder and disintegrate into the nothingness of the too-white walls. It seemed like a futile exercise, and Raj was glad to see Ibti's vibrant green eyes glance around the bedroom door.

—Don't bother too much with that, love. Just relax tonight. Before you go.

—Ach, I just wanted to get a bit done, y'know. Feel guilty as it is, leaving.

—Raj, I'm not popping anytime soon. Just go. And be careful.

—Not sure what we're even doing, to be honest.

—Well, you can stay and watch birth partner vids with me instead then.

—God, they're shite, eh.

—Hey, if I can get a back massage out if it...

Raj smiled at Ibti as she slinked back around the narrow

corridor in her loose black pantsuit and headed towards the exercise ball in the small square living area overlooking cranes and KFC and, in the distance, a murky bend of the River Thames. For all his love and well-meaning articulations of guilt about swanning off to Skye, Raj was feeling more fragile about his ongoing numbness towards impending fatherhood than he was about leaving Ibti. It was the unexpected anaesthesia of it all. It was unsettling. No dread nor excitement, no fear nor quiet confidence. Nothing. Just a dull acknowledgement of what many call a miracle. The thought of Ibti glowing, happy, and plump in belly kept him going; but it had little to do with fatherhood or facing the unprecedented flurry of first times that are supposed to be exciting or scary or special or... something. He didn't really feel much at all.

Raj fell back on the floor, supporting himself with one arm and using the other to gently spray a star-stencil banner onto the left shoulder of his black slim-fit shirt. It disintegrated to a stain of faded particles that would probably never wash away. He wouldn't be wearing it to any more PR meetings at Whitehall. Tracing the outline of five forgotten points, he remembered the red stars he used to sew into vintage army jackets back at uni; the lively pride with which he espoused communism, anti-fascism and *realpolitik!* in the face of disinterested peers and pub-goers.

Raj brushed over the snowy particles with a nervous index finger, unsure if his guttural recoil was shaped by retrospective naïvety or a shrinking inability to reconcile his past self with who he was now. Shared homeowner in a gentrifying suburb of South London; financially secure; tenured to Her Majesty's government; married to a brilliant middle-class Brazilian immigration lawyer engaged in social justice struggles from the NGO ivory tower of a Regent's Park mansion. And now... soon-to-be father. Only the latter news had sparked unrepentant flashbacks. A pining for the irretrievable past. A hazy mist causing a cold in his soul. A malady of longing to feel life like you once did whilst simultaneously spluttering at the person who felt it.

Raj ruminated as the particles faded and freckled and streaked. A verse he once read by the Spanish mystic and poet St. John of the Cross came to mind. It described – as Raj thought, at least – some kind of temporary spiritual crisis. An emotional vacuum that was necessary for one to live through before the birth of a new belief, bond, or perhaps being:

> *In an obscure night*
> *Fevered with love's anxiety*
> *(O hapless, happy plight!)*
> *I went, none seeing me*
> *Forth from my house, where all things quiet be*

The sound of crushed ice avalanched into the room and Raj wiped his shirt clean. Ibti, his sublimation, called into the wilderness from the small square living area.

—Raj, come through. Made you a marg. Even did a non-alcoholic one for me!

—Thanks, ma love. You're right. Let's make a night of it. I'm gonna miss yi.

DR ROBERT MILNE (BOBBY)

Raj arrived to find Bobby creased into a dusty brown bean cushion, thoughtfully stroking the ivory horn vessel that nestled into his coarse chest.

—Aye aye, Bobby.

—Arite.

—Nice horn.

—Am I gien yi the horn?

—Nit.

Raj wasn't taken aback by the bearded, bean-bagged, half-naked being before him. Even though it had been a couple of years. Even though he was sipping from an ivory horn.

Even though his pungent single-skinner was uncomfortably Proustian. The mood between them was relaxed. The type of relaxed only possible among estranged friends whose past overrides the necessity for polite conversation. Teuchter greetings helped temper reunion formalities. Raj had always thought of these customary utterances – "Arite, min?" "Phoos yer doos?" "Like en?" – as uncanny markers of familiarity in unfamiliar circumstances. He imagined it might have been the way nineteenth-century emigrants greeted new arrivals; ushered off the boat with words and vowels that burred beyond estrangement, before a more lucid slip between registers emerged.

—Is that actually an ivory horn?

—Aye.

—Thought you were vegetarian?

—It's a cup, nae a burrito.

Bobby had found the ivory horn in a charity shop up the West End a few weeks ago. He frowned through his circular wood-frames for approximately twenty-five seconds before buying it, twizzling the stray ends of his beard as he contemplated the ethics of the purchase. He thought of a gaunt, moustached viceroy plundering the object from some Rajasthani villager, and an imperial policeman shooting the elephant. But it was dead now. They were dead now. The horn was here now – and so was he. It would be a good re-useable cup. Much better than the bamboo ones from the organic supermarket. It might even make the do-gooders who bought them reconsider notions of primitivism and progress and time and ethics; and make them realise that their great-great-great grandfather should have left that Rajasthani villager alone. After those twenty-five seconds of contemplation, he nodded approvingly, bought it, and strolled across to Costa for a frothy pumpkin latte, spiced with cumin.

Bobby's ivory horn rested, when not dangling from his wide neck, on a custom-built wooden cradle placed on the centre his living-room mantlepiece. Just above it, there was a framed picture of a cartoon octopus in a gentleman's top hat, sitting on top of a gentleman's top hat. Its tentacles were slathering around the regal man's ears and mutton chops. Raj was curious.

—S'at, like?

—Octopus? Ah up in eh boy's heid, like.

—Aye.

—Nae pint in fichtin it!

—Aye, righto. Okay, Bobby.

Much had happened since the last time Raj and Bobby met. That had been after an intensive week of therapy in the psychiatric ward at Queen Margaret's Hospital, which Bobby now preferred to call by a more nineteenth-century name: the Royal Lunatic Asylum of Scotland. He felt "lunatic" afforded a charismatic gravitas lost to an overly polite modernity, and he was comfortable now, even proud, to have a handle on his self, health, and personal history. It was different to the days when intrusive thoughts dictated his mind, body, and every move. He'd come a long way: steadied by CBT, Krishna Das, magic circle meet-ups, badminton, and turning to a plant-based diet. Except bacon ("because bacon is cultural and ca be replaced") and fish ("because Kurt Cobain said they didn't have any feelings in 'Something in the Way'").

Bobby sprung from his dusty brown beanbag with the gait of a large but technically proficient gymnast. Despite his large frame, he moved with acumen and purpose. He looked leaner than Raj remembered.

—Lookin trim, min.

—Aye. The Chinese.

—Phit?

—The Chinese. Chinese International Students' Badminton Society.

—Phit are you on?

—Badminton wi the Chinese international students. Need to be quicker than a ninja.

—Bit racist, Bobby?

—Da put me doon with yer politically correct posturin. Yer better. But aye. Am jokin. Nae think ah ken Ninjas were covert mercenaries in feudal Japan. Nithin much adee with the Qing dynasty. If onything, ma self-conscious conflation o ethnicities and cultural stereotypes wiz merely a nod towards the stupidity of ithers. So, aye, keep yer highminded posturing in yer pipe and smoke it.

—Righto, Bobby.

Bobby performed some form of faux tai chi gesture with his hands before turning towards the small open-plan kitchen area adjoining his living room in one swift pirouette. An army marches on its belly, he assured Raj, so he'd got the messages in for breakfast.

—Bacon bap for now and a rowie for the road?

—Aye, Bobby, that would be good.

They finished breakfast, picked up their bags, and left the flat. A few seconds out the door, Bobby stopped in his tracks and about-turned, prompting a confused look from Raj.

—Where yi goin now, min?

—Forgot something.

VIDHUSHEI YOGESWARAN (VIDDY)

The twins vaulted macaroni at each other's rabid faces before slumbering. Viddy left them blanketed, asleep, and crept out the back door of the croft. She listened to the lambs' spluttery hunger-moans, burst dew bubbles on the mossy bricks, and allowed the crisp air of silage to sour her nostrils. She found glimmers of peace on bright Skye mornings like these. It was eighteen months since John's accident. The ropey python lashing his ankles. Blue lights swirling the croft. The analogue crackle of that Radio Scotland headline.

> A crewman on a creel boat died after his leg became entangled in fishing gear and he was dragged overboard, accident investigators have said.

It was dead now. He was dead now. She was here now – and so were the twins. She had been doing some writing in these brief moments of respite from the yelps of Adeepa and Angus, and even considered producing some kind of memoir with a marketable back cover:

> Born in London to Tamil refugees, journalist turned crofter Vidhushei Yogeswaran was raised in Scotland and had always felt a sense of otherness. When her husband

tragically dies in a fishing accident, Yogeswaran embarks on a trip around the Isle of Skye, delving through layers of memory, language, and natural history to try and come to terms with her grief. With an unusual but timely eco-spiritual edge, and an alluring blend of memoir and nature writing, this powerful read touches on themes of identity, belonging, and loss, as it charts how a recently bereaved, restless spirit puts her next foot forward in life.

But the thought of profiting creatively, financially, or therapeutically in any way from John's death, from trauma, and from making other trauma-survivors feel small in the face of a glossy paperback, made her wince. Besides, she cringed at all those books written by over-privileged arseholes who commodified the healing powers of travel, nature, forest bathing, foraging, and Romantic Scotland, and had little sense of their own entitlement. How wonderful it would be for us all to *heal in nature*, apparently unencumbered by time, money, dirty nappies, spew, and tantrums. It induced her own tantrum. Her own spew. She knew it was irrational. Probably just jealous. She was nowhere near ready to face up to herself that way. Face outwards that way. Face inwards that way. And that was okay.

Caring for Adeepa and Angus was enough for now, and they also provided shelter from the well-meaning support of her friends in the Skye Craft and Wild Swim Collective. The candlelit vigil they organised in Staffin; daily visits from Freya; yoga groups; tea parties; sympathetic smiles; knitwear for the twins; wild swims; help with the cows; muffins; teacakes; cards; more knitwear for the twins; more wild swims; and more... could they all just fuck off for a minute? Empathy was asphyxia, and she just wanted to breathe in the silage alone. John never really liked the SCWSC much anyway. He was from Strontian, Ardnamurchan, and was no more Sgiathanach than the rest of them. But he didn't share their university backgrounds, woke sensibilities, champagne socialism, and penchant for oversized knitwear and ethereal electronica. Fishing was just what he did, what he had always done. It wasn't some political statement about climate or sustainability or libertarianism. He wasn't interested in posting pictures of himself cleaning up cow shit to make friends in the city marvel at the dirt under his nails. And it was this sense of himself that Viddy loved most, but also what made some of her older friendships hard to maintain.

She thought of the time John met Raj, Bobby, and Liam back in... when was it now, 2008? It felt like an unstated ending, a sobering up from the haze of youthful energy that intoxicated them through the previous few years. Student hols, India, library binges, arguing, drinking, grieving, mourning, Valium, laughing, getting high. All that seemed far off, naïve, immature that day. Most of the boozy lunch was taken up by Raj awkwardly asking John about life on a fishing boat. Nobody was comfortable, everybody was tipsy, and mutual bellows – "Great to finally meet you!" "Aye, can't believe it's taken us this long!" "Was great seeing you again!" "Safe trip back to the island!" echoed around a dusky Ashton Lane as they hugged and parted ways, relieved, hollow, nervous, a little sad.

In time, a warmer nostalgia superseded sadness. But Viddy was still anxious, or excited, or maybe an unsettling combination of both. She rested her head against the mossy croft wall and started laughing. She laughed louder, combing her fingers through thick black hair in some strange, nostalgic relief. The thought of Liam hungover and ill-equipped for the weather, in gutties; Raj pretending he was way more outdoorsy than he was; and the likelihood of Bobby showing up in 1890s deerstalker garb for his "Highland Tour". Preposterous.

The twins were grumbling, so Viddy slipped back inside, patchwork gown flailing in the wind behind. She needed to get them dressed, packed, and write a list for Freya of what they needed to eat.

LIAM MCMANAMAN

Liam leafed through the back pages of the *Daily Record* in the corner of the Dalmuir Diner. He cut an oddly elegant figure – cross-legged, slick black hair, lean leather jacket – and might be vulnerable if it were not for the radiant, edgy confidence that kept the burly workies at bay. It had been a tiring few days, and he needed the greasy decompression – coffee, full breakfast, paper, old hen patter – before heading over to James's garage in Drumry.

The diner had become something of a morning ritual since he'd moved back to renovate, but today the faint clangs of cutlery and fragmented grill sizzles were particularly therapeutic. Liam's mum, Rhona, had been done for breach of the peace earlier in the week. It was a good outcome, and he was glad the debacle was over. One of their neighbours in Bearsden had, apparently, been taking photos of children from his window, taps aff, as spotted by Liam's wee sister, Ashlene. Rhona's reaction, somewhere between measured and red mist, was to turn up on his door and beat his mouth bloody with a black stiletto. Knowing who she was, and who her sons were, the man's red lips remained sealed about the beating, and she got off with a minor public disturbance. Liam smiled to himself, thinking about James's initial reaction to it.

—Yi can take the girl oota Drumchapel, eh...

Liam feigned a laugh but felt uneasy that Ashlene, just eleven years old and sole witness to the lewd photographer, had developed a habit of lying compulsively in recent weeks.

Moving back had been hard. Liam felt guilty for feeling the oppression of familial love. He'd felt closer to them all when their relationship was less defined by physical location and more by the memories and imagined bonds which became real in times of mutual need, happiness, even tragedy. Nowadays their paths were intersecting in spatial arrangements that infringed upon his sense of freedom and identity. Though it was hard to know what those things even meant anymore. An unnerving vulnerability simmered beneath Liam's performative confidence; a confidence that had always paved his rambunctious way forward in life. In fact, there was a creeping sense that the very need to perform, to seem authentic and rebelliously true, had left him lagging behind.

To be true to oneself, if such a thing as personal truths exists, meant – for Liam, at least – maintaining the narrative of a rebellious self. And that was a hard bargain, particularly when it came to conceding the transmigrations and narrative ruptures of the old ghosts dancing around his own spirit. Raj's well-paid job, Bobby's recovery groups, Viddy's kids – and then there was Liam. The sad last rebel. Childless, jobless, and eating cheap diner breakfasts funded by black-market motorcycle sales. Surely free will should amount to something more than becoming a parody of a person intent on exerting free will?

It was good to have the Dalmuir Diner to mull this over on a daily basis. Clanging cutlery, echoes of older ghosts.

Perhaps they would make him smile again. Remind him of who he was or who he might want to be now. James was doing him a good turn anaw.

The jangle of Liam's knife and fork against the crimson-streaked plate broke his reverie. He should make tracks.

Liam arrived at the garage to find James's stout figure hunched under the bonnet of a rusty red Fiesta. Tanned orange, six foot three, blackened hands, bald head, boiler suit, neck tattoos – James was imposing, but a bright flash of white teeth quickly turned intimidation to charm.

—Awrite, wee bro, off on adventures again, eh? Quite right, ma man.

—Aye, bruv. When yi comin along?

—Am no sure am cut oot fur bongs under a banyan tree these days.

—Were yi ever?

—Aye, mate, yi missed ma hippy days. Lang hair, spliffs, and aw that.

—That before or aifter yi started tyin cunts up in the forest?

—Ssshht, wee yin. Ah wiz no saint, but am no proud o it either.

—Aw the reason to hit a wee bong under a banyan tree, bruv!

James was full of admiration for his wee brother's way of winging it; out the scheme, Glasgow uni, ashrams in India, yoga in South America. He would do anything for Liam, including, most recently, helping to restore and sell old motorcycles that were being shipped over from Mumbai. Between the part-time charity gig, canvassing, and renovating old council flats in the Drum, it was just another one of Liam's turns that allowed him to float on without a full-time job, free to up sticks to an ashram or meditation retreat whenever he felt the whim. It was a well-rehearsed form of free will, but also a well-loved act most of the time.

But recently it had all become a little tiring. This performance.

James walked his younger brother over to the three Royal Enfield Bullets.

THE ROYAL ENFIELD BULLET

The Royal Enfield Bullet.

Indian?

British?

Or Anglo-Indian? A term that "refers to at least two groups: those with mixed Indian and British ancestry and those of British descent born or living in India". No, the primary focus on "Anglo" sounds too *English*. And it's not like these machines were born out of some harmonious union that transcended imperial culture, capitalistic gain, and exploitation. But we tend to forget about that in love and lust and sex and death and riding around pretending we have free will on the *the oldest global motorcycle brand in continuous production.*

Global.

That most nebulous of illusions that makes it sound like people across cultures can belong together. But where? The ghosts of those Bangladeshi border corpses might have something to say about the *global* merits of a machine that buzzed the Border Security Force around as they papped out rounds and cleansed their new country of veil and scripture and calls to prayer.

Strange how something *so British* could become *so Indian.*

So militantly Indian.

And still the Republic Day Daredevils ride Enfields on

their heads and loop and toot and shoot to celebrate the collapse of crown rule whilst simultaneously revving up their own yoke of tyranny, home, and Hinduism. Hard to know who to be sometimes. Especially in a new home. Globally exhausting.

So, anyway, to sustain this song of freedom, let's just say that the Royal Enfield is made up of some British parts, its birthplace is in Chennai, and its spiritual home is the Himalayas, where the wheels seem to lift and levitate above the rocky terrain that cuts up, down, and around hemp-smelling hills that swirl in supernatural wonder. It's a strange term, though, "spiritual home", as if everyone has some place to go to appease their spirit, find their sense of self.

For surely there's a great tyranny in binding a person or thing to a physical place. The question is not "How" nor "Who" nor "When" but *Where* is your home? What an oppression.

An existential crisis in a "local" café you have come to hate. Arriving in a new town to "build a home" only to be smacked with regret. Moving "away" then missing "home" to the point of petrification.

What a tyranny. What an oppression.

Swimming eyes. Tortured fragility. Weary loneliness.

An old song from the "homeland" played on a broken violin by a broken man who left home and could never return. Like all the old songs. Like all the old broken men. Like all the longing.

All this is exhausting. This tyranny.

It certainly begs questions about "spirit" and "home" and "imagination". It begs questions, too, about whether machines might also need, like humans, a sense of journey, transcendence, and community to exist with any purpose.

An imagined place where they belong – not by birth or nation or blood or bolt – but by virtue of myth, narrative, song, and imagination. Perhaps this is some small salvation: the idea that we might share our predicament with objects and machines in mutual wonder, mutual crises.

This is particularly true of the lost and weary legs which were, and will, sooner or later, be wrapped around Royal Enfield Bullets in search of a song to sing for themselves.

There is a great salience in listening out for these songs.

Songs that allow for the silences, murmurs, and offbeat syncopations of undefined relationships. Relationships that run parallel to, or even apart from, family, politics, sex, and love; forged by that irrepressible human instinct that binds us to ornament, art, and machine. We leave them, return to them, leave them again, then return and take for granted the perpetual "home" provided by a world that transcends love and lust and skin.

It's hard to know where the Royal Enfield Bullet really belongs or who it belongs to. But it has powerful notions. Powerful imaginings. Beyond borders. Beyond nations. Beyond our world.

Perhaps we all have the capacity for this. These notions that fade to silence in the clamour of the human world.

The tyranny of home, or the torment of who and where one belongs, then, can only be healed from within.

This was true of the pale-brown-skinned (or brown-pale-skinned) children left behind by regal East India Company merchants in purple flowing gowns and bejewelled turbans.

This is true, too, of the Royal Enfield Bullet, and its companions.

The Kirtankara.

THE

KIRTAN

IS THIS WHAT YOU WANTED?

What are estranged
friends if not ghosts? Real ghosts
aren't dead people. Dead people haunt our
memories, our minds, our strengths, our regrets,
our aspirations – but they haunt from a lifeless place.
The life they had is over, fragmented into ethers which might
join with other ethers to make something new one day. And so their
hauntings are always partial, fragmented, a dim murmur of imagination.
They comfort us, sadden us, please us, but rarely frightens us – because
life has transformed, and we know they can't return. Not like real ghosts.
Real ghosts operate in a space where the over and done with is always apt
to return. Where the possibilities of another past haunt our present or
threaten our future. Where absent presences disrupt our sensibilities
and send us into frenzies of indecision about who we are and who we
once were. These ghosts aren't dead people; nor are they apparitions,
wailing ghouls, screeching banshees, or befallen creatures trapped
in an unrequited search for vengeance. These ghosts are old
friends. We pass real ghosts every day; they haunt others who
we'll never meet or know. We all live in houses that are
haunted. By the ghosts of ourselves. Them and us.
Is this what we wanted? The Kirtankara
sing, dance, fall silent,
and sing again.

It was 2008 when things first started to change. Each of them felt the entropic fragmentation of friendship, inevitable and disorientating. Liam was increasingly absent, moving in different circles, and he had developed a habit – at least, that's how they saw it. He was trying to convince Raj to stay around the West End to make a mint off selling weed to undergraduates. It was easy money. Liam had the contacts, and Raj could be the link to the off-kilter haircut creatives. But Raj had other ideas. There was a clash of sensibilities, potentially class, potentially cultures. Raj was moving to Berlin to study photography part-time and live out his boho-barista dreams. Money was a worry, as were the pressures of ever finding a "proper job" given his Oedipal rejection of law, medicine, and rising to meet the paternal demands of caste in the imperial metropole.

Viddy felt similar anxieties, but she was, and always had been, happier in her own skin. She was spending more time at a co-operative allotment in the Southside than with the others, and planned to WWOOF around farms for a while, learning, growing, learning how to grow, and living for herself instead of for others.

Amidst organic vegetable allotments and Berlin squats, Liam felt adrift. He was tired and fatigued by the increasingly flaky realm of liberal cosmopolitanism that surrounded him; a realm that once seduced him into thinking he could be something, or someone else. He began to feel detached from his life at uni, which, in retrospect, seemed increasingly like an ideological bubble that he was forced into by the establishment. A bubble people like him should be trying to burst, not float around in before crashing back unconscious in the harmless gutters of passivity and getting pissed. Passive. Harmless. Back in place. It was all too much. For want of a better way to articulate himself – actually, perhaps it was the best way – he needed to get tae fuck. So, he got tae fuck. Oot his nut. Brown. Green. Carlos Vallies. But it couldn't last.

Bobby was the most composed of them all that year, deciding to extend his undergraduate research project into a Masters, which led to a PhD on *The Literary and Cultural History of the Potato in Aberdeenshire c.1845–1848*. His argument hinged on the historical neglect of the effects of the potato famine in North-East Scotland, and he mostly enjoyed those years spent researching and writing about the price of oatmeal and tatties to the crackling sounds of bothy ballads. The work had purpose. He dug with his pen. He felt close to his people.

Sadly, his efforts were misunderstood and much ridiculed by his friends back in the Shire. It started in jest and, at first, he wore the title of "Doc Tattie" with a smile, even felt a little pride in it. But it wore thin, especially coming from overpaid, red-faced rigger pals with fat necks and fatter wallets. It was hard. They had little understanding of scholarship or folklore or anything beyond the fact that it was daft that Bobby had chosen to pursue something that didn't make money. How would he ever get his Audi, mortgage, and second mortgage? Wankers. Bobby felt torn. Would they ever understand the deconstructivist underpinnings of his scholarship and capacity for deep philosophical concepts? Probably not. Rig pigs. Ach. That was too judgemental on the brethren. So, regardless, Bobby committed to ancestral songs of the soil, to stoicism, and to the strange conservatism that emanates from generations of Picts who became generations of Presbyterians who became generations of dour pricks. He embraced the frosty silences, frowny nods, and the perceived "honest worth o it a". His ancestors spoke to him. Jimmy MacBeath growling "Hey Barra Gadgie" on Granda Duthie's old records; Bennachie sunsets; and young fairmers spewin outside the Belmont chipper on a Saturday night in shite cheque shirts. The sincere humility of it all. People don't have to *make* the Deen; they don't have to pretend to be the "friendliest city in the world" – they just are. Weegies, min. Burring vowels and big egos and nae sincerity, nae substance. Funny cunts, though.

Raj had a different experience growing up in the North-East. He made some good friends – Bobby, Duncan – but always felt dislocated. His ancestral soil and songs were elsewhere, or nowhere. Conversations with Bobby over the years about colonialism and kinship made him reflect on the reasons for this spiritual vacuum; an inability to connect family with place. Raj's mother, Morag, was a native Gaelic speaker who grew up in Oban and moved to Glasgow where she met his dad, Vishal. She followed him, Raj plump in her belly, up to the North-East where he worked at Aberdeen Royal Infirmary. Raj didn't speak the native tongue of either parent, let alone know their ancestral songs. And his restlessness, his discontent, was just a manifestation of longing to be somewhere else, without knowing where. Bobby, in all his intellectual nuance, was one of the few friends who understood this, which explains why they formed such a bond in the latter years of high school; smoking, playing music together, and eventually going on to study degrees in Glasgow – Bobby opting for history and Raj English.

The move to Glasgow offered Raj a sense of belonging, for a while. He was closer to the Gàidhealtachd and, while he still didn't understand the songs, he felt warmth in the echoes of The Park Bar and Islay Inn, and also enjoyed better Indian food and bigger Asian communites without ever being part of them. He found his own people for a while. It was Bobby who introduced Raj to Viddy, who also studied history, and Raj started to bring Liam along to the pub after English classes. The four of them got close quickly. A swift coalescence of friendship that rarely occurs outside the intensity of shared new collective experience in tender or transitory moments. A swift coalescence that feels magic, tingly; an ecstasy of the mundane, immediately etched into our forever-consciousness, forever-memory, unlike the sum of our day-to-day coming and goings. A rare friendship. A ship that would soon sail.

It was just a year after meeting they decided – on a whim, drunk in The Arlington, The Maytals' "It's You I Love" pulping bassy under their shouty conversation – to splurge their student loans on a trip to India the following summer. They all wanted to find something, somewhere else. Together.

Curls of tobacco-stained wallpaper crusted across the floor of the musty flat. Rain chattered against a single-glazed window. White paint cracked across four square frames divided by a cold brass lever with several little holes in it, each encircled in a crown of rust. There was much left to do but Liam was done for the day. He collapsed back, uncrumpling his bag of chips on the sofa-bed, which lay sparse and lonely and fragile like an island. He closed his eyes in a moment of great weariness that fast became one of great ceremony when Leonard Cohen appeared promising dawns and morning afters. It had been a while. Liam clicked the little + button on the tinny speakers, recrumpled the soggy grey paper, and spread out as if he were someone else. Then, closing his eyes, he returned to what he once was, or what he dreamed he once was, or still was, perhaps.

In the beautiful desolation of a Gumtree sofa-bed, imperfectly circled in ceremonial flakes, Liam remembered everything. The clarity of a dirt road cutting through drooping quilts of cloud. Plump green bushes that swirled with supernatural wonder in his corner vision. And that Himalayan eagle. For one brief or forever moment, an eagle was gliding beside him, its talons mirroring his own curling grasp around the warm, rubbery, vibrating throttle. And in the corner of a tobacco-stained room and on a dirt road, everything became meaningless. Was this what he wanted? To live in a house that was haunted? The eagle, the memory, the feeling, and the forgetting seemed to become one – all bound up with the backache caused by a shite Gumtree bed and the faint patter of rain against fragile windowpanes.

Liam opened his eyes and glanced around the room with the weariness of one forced to acknowledge a world long dead. The crumpled, soggy chip paper fell into confetti as he pulled himself upright and over to the window, loosening the rusty brass lever to let in the whispering draft of raindrops. A grey dusk befell the red fun-slide across the street, which was dwarfed by three high-rises in the distance, diagonally adjacent to one another. It was an image he had seen before he had seen it, in that very moment, yet he gazed ahead with sustained intensity and intrigue. In between the foregrounded fun-slide and horizonal high-rises, a narrow concrete path snaked below a row of shops.

UCanSave Newsagents. Nicolann's Hair Salon.
PowerBet88.

Beside them, or perhaps underneath them, an old man was ambling along the path. One shoulder hunched higher than the other, padded steel walking stick strewn out to right his balance. Liam watched the rain patter off the old man's flatcap and long brown duffel coat, which seemed resplendent, damp, glossy. The old man didn't seem to have any purpose, nor care about getting wet. He walked without intent, and seemed to symbolise nothing, which was why he was so significant. He was going nowhere and had never been anybody and belonged to the rain and the fun-slide and the horizonal high-rises and that moment. To be and to feel these things again, Liam thought. There was a small joy in the clean clarity of this episode. Liam felt a new promise of dawn in the bleak darkening of day. Tomorrow, he would go to the Dalmuir Diner and call Raj. It had been too long.

It *had* been too long. But it felt strange to reach out to that lifeless place which had, no doubt, been replaced by so much... life. Old friendships, times past, life-less. Life was elsewhere. Liam's gaze fixed upon the luminous body of a bluebottle which halted momentarily on the edge of the cracked white window frame. He wondered where it might have flown (did they visit lots of places in their lives?) before it chose, for some reason, to be still, in that moment. But this was just a distraction from the fear. Liam was scared of returning to that lifeless place only to find out he never existed at all. Even worse, he was scared that he still didn't exist; always pretending to be someone, living unthinkingly, grasping around for whatever physical entities of identity were best suited to the fluid interests of his pride, ego, and exterior representation. The luminous bluebottle rapidly buzzed off the cracked white frame into nothingness.

Liam looked around the room. Torn, tobacco-stained wallpaper, Gumtree sofa, crumpled bag of chips, and a few SNP leaflets he'd promised to deliver for the local councillor who'd taken quite a shine to him. Liam "had what it takes", she told him, to "stir up all sorts of communities again". He could "capture the minds", she said, "of the folks they missed last time around". Try and get them to "dream about a nation free from Tory tyranny". With instinctual gusto, Liam excitedly agreed, but his motivation had seeped far from the sanguine hopes he held in 2014. Politics felt like a flash affair for him; impassioned holiday sex a few summers back that had very quickly turned into pissing with the toilet door open before bed in the hope of a quickie. He thought of Birte's wildness; she was the bespectacled German exchange student and copy editor of the pamphlet *Socialist Scotland: Now!* She left the country in all its failed radicalism shortly after they romped around the Highlands together on a whim, full of whisky, optimism, and good sex.

She was probably a conservative intern in Hamburg by now, pissing with the toilet door open opposite a stock exchange banker named Wolfgang. Meanwhile people like him – or, rather, people from places like his – were left to struggle, unaided by a shitty welfare state and with even shittier prospects for real, meaningful change. At least they could dream though, eh, thought Liam. But maybe that was part of the problem. So much time spent navel-gazing about utopian ideals that every cunt seemed to forget they were inside their own tiny belly button, trapped inside an insular wee passage that led right through to their tightly shut and contented arsehole, south of the body. Jesus Christ, man. It was hard for Liam to remember himself. Or, rather, to dream how to be.

The immediate meaningless of this all was at once terrifying and liberating.

Tomorrow, he would go to the Dalmuir Diner and call Raj.

It had been too long.

In the light mist of a spring Monday morning, Raj sat smoking under a cosmological sculpture in the British Library Piazza. The courtyard was coming to life with book-laden, backpacked visitors as the early turmoil of the Euston Road traffic sounded busy but obscure in the distance. Raj's Canon camera swung left as he tilted, squinted, and craned his neck towards the imperfect circle of eight igneous rocks inscribed with little human figures. *Planets*. He pondered. Some sculptural evocation of knowledge and elemental presence? Human futility in the wake of glacial and spatial magnitudes? Pretty, but the sculpture seemed to perpetuate these Eurocentric notions of knowledge that were increasingly bothering him.

On lunch breaks and after photo shoots, Raj was spending time in the India Office Records archive, which he chanced upon with great intrigue whilst shooting promos for the library's upcoming initiative to decolonise its collections. On Wednesday past, he'd found a nineteenth-century document called *The Cosmological Beliefs of The Gondi Peoples*. The Gondi (*obviously*, now that he thought about it) had astronomical conceptions, nomenclatures, and perspectives void of any external influence (why *would* they care about Roman Gods like Jupiter?). Most striking was the extent to which these conceptions stretched beyond the mythologies and spiritualities associated with "Eastern" traditions. Sun was *Din*. Moon was *Chandal*. Moon was *Jango*. Sun was *Lingo*. But none of that mattered anymore. It hadn't done for hundreds of years. Raj exhaled and watched little clouds of smoke rise then dissipate and disappear.

It was one of the more interesting gigs for the Department of Culture, Media and Sport; a promotional campaign that was to document "national" and "institutional" efforts to "confront the colonial legacies of the past". Yet, unexpectedly, it threw Raj off balance, jolted his professional pragmatism, and sent him spiralling into periods of self-searching, as if some ancestor inside him was demanding answers. The shoot itself was an easy gig; photographing old books, archives, paintings, antiquities, and all those other things that came to constitute perceptions of other places by those who were never from those places in the first place, whatever "the first place" was. But the irony of Raj capturing authoritative new images of these things and re-presenting them to "the world" grated on him, leading to an increasingly fraught feeling towards the project, and himself.

Amidst the prospect of rearing a child in this fragile world, Raj found himself questioning his own moves to innocence over the years. Born with the curse and boon of being both Scottish *and* mixed race, it was hard to know how to be. Or how he should be seen to be now. He would likely buy her (they knew from Ibti's insistence on an early scan) a Scotland 1974 World Cup sleep suit. But she would have to learn about the futility of a nation being simultaneously the oppressed and never the oppressor. They would likely celebrate Diwali. But she would have to learn that her high-caste Punjabi grandfather should not be used to mark her own heritage and history as blameless in processes of racial discrimination and colonial subjugation. Raj was, perhaps, searching too hard for mercy in the white-passing face of his own mirror. A mirror that reminded him, each morning, that he was soon to be a father in a world that weighed heavy. This was a difficult reality. It was hard to know how to be. Who to be. Where to be.

When Raj and Ibti first met, it was their rootlessness that entwined them; disparate strands and wayward experiences paradoxically bound through the early haze of love, lust, and discovery. Ibtisam grew up in São Paulo. She was born to a vivacious and resilient Eritrean mother who was granted asylum, and an intellectual Brazilian father whose kindness never ceased. The deep chasm left by her father's death from cancer was partly what led Ibti to move away for a Masters in Immigration Law at the University of Amsterdam, before an internship in The Hague, then a full-time gig in London. She and Raj met at a weekly film night in Brixton that screened cult classics and arthouse flicks to raise money for asylum seekers whose official status was still pending. Smiles over wine and *L'Atalante* one week led to laughter over sushi and *Tokyo Story* the next; while a drunken night of Macunaíma cocktails gave Raj the courage to ask if she wanted to go for walk in Regent's Park at the weekend. They spent the whole weekend together, slept little, then went camping in Cornwall the following weekend following a hazy train ride full of wonder, curiosity, interlocking legs, hip-flask swigs, blurry trees, blurrier glances, and kisses. They fast became each other's home, unbound by place, nation, even language. Their longing to be placeless, so often the cause of previous break-ups and relationship flakes, was what united them. The possibilities of where they might go was unnerving and limitless. A sublime state of belonging to nowhere and each other. They decided to call it love.

There was a brief period when Raj and Ibti considered moving up to Scotland on a more permanent basis, when momentum was picking up around 2014. It seemed exciting to Ibti; a revolutionary energy, or the possibility of a socialist ideal they both – at some point or other – dreamed of. Raj was more sceptical but subdued his opinions for fear of seeming out of step with his friends back home (Liam was even campaigning!) and the liberally minded masses. Raj never really believed that there was *actually* a liberally minded mass; but rather an artful *construction* of a liberally minded mass. A mass that seemed foreign, unknown, and fictional to him and the sum of his experiences. And his father's experiences.

—Dunno, Ibti. It's not some left-wing utopia, y'know? Like, you sometimes talk about London being small-minded, even a bit racist in some ways... Well, I bet if we moved...

—Raj! It's the energy, though. It seems so refreshing. Be cool to be amongst that just now, no?

—Aye, maybe. But it'll pass. Whatever way it goes. It'll pass. And then we might wonder why we moved. I just don't know.

The moment passed and so did the utopian visions, as well as their idea to move. There had been brief mentions of São Paulo, too. Raj could freelance for the advertising agencies there. Language wasn't so much of a problem when pictures sold his stories, but the cost of living was too high. And it would be too weird for Ibti to go back. A sad defeat. And, so, the years passed. Exploited by landlords in Brixton. Camberwell co-ops. Permanent jobs and, finally, their own little place in Deptford, baby on the way. Suddenly London had become home, and it felt – to Raj, at least – like their newbuild tower block was standing paralysed in the middle of a gentrified snare that could, at any moment, squeeze the life out of the people around them, as well as their love.

Raj exhaled. The smoke lingered long in air, rising above the planets, little people, and scurrying scholars that began to appear then disappear. This was probably all Oedipal anyway. This apparent refusal to embrace England – or was it Britain? A quest to kill the colonial mindset of a father who remained adamant *they* brought railways and education and an enlightened form of rule that differed from those barbaric hothead Spaniards.

He stubbed out his cigarette on a black shadow cast by one of the igneous rocks. Today's shoot was short; archival holdings of books, manuscripts, and objects related to "snake charming", in all their conceptions or misconceptions. An intellectual inquest to root out the plunder and platitudes of loot once disguised as mutual exchange. Or something like that. He would be finished by noon and planned to consult the papers of Donald Friell McLeod later, which he had chanced upon a day earlier. It was a ghostly reminder of a place and past he was wholly unsure actually existed. So strange to learn that the village he and his uni friends visited all those years ago was named after this "Exalted Star of India". So strange. So ghostly. They had no idea. A Highlander in Himalayan hills hundreds of years before them. All gaunt, high cheekbones and books and learning and misplaced sympathy for forgotten Gondi knowledges. How did they not realise it all back then?

So strange. So ghostly.

Raj exhaled. Smaller clouds, more clarity.

His phone buzzed around in his back pocket. Liam was calling. It had been a while.

So strange. So ghostly.

Bobby woke early in a sudden tangle of confusion and slumped into his dusty brown bean cushion in an incomprehensible state of tedium. With his waking was born several wants. For the vicarious seduction of travel, an epic journey, a bacon bap, some rowies, and a frothy pumpkin latte spiced with cumin. But he was too tired to venture. The vast spectacle of travels past and future continued to fill Bobby's mind with a wave of brilliant tedium as he dreamed his morning brown bean cushion dream and slowly roused to a consciousness filled with contradictory thoughts.

To travel you just need to exist. Aye, he thought. In the bean cushion of my body, I lean out and over and look back and forwards. Old friends and new faces are always the same but always looking different, as is the way with all familiar landscapes from a train window and dusty brown bean cushion. Aye. If I imagine the place, I can be there. The futility of travel when I can feel it all from here! Paris, Punjab, Beinn Dorain – where else would I be but inside myself? What I've seen was not what I saw but who I am. And still am. Still here. In my dusty brown bean cushion. Aye. Fucksake, it's boring though. And I miss my old friends. Could really do with a bacon bap and frothy pumpkin latte spiced with cumin instead of just thinking about them.

Bobby rifled through the messily stacked pile of vinyls and 12" sleeves in the upcycled cabinet to his left, which was, most conveniently, within dusty brown bean cushion reaching distance. It was a radius he'd measured with precision and great purpose amidst the surprising intoxication of masculinity that comes with sawing up old pallet boards. The damp flop of vinyl against vinyl fell to silence as he came upon that iconic cover image for *New Skin*; a woodcut from the alchemical *Rosarium philosophorum*, or "Rosary of the Philosophers". Whilst studying for his PhD, some years after their India trip, Bobby learned that there was an original manuscript copy held at the University of Glasgow's Special Collections department. It was a welcome distraction from the price of nineteenth-century oatmeal, and led to a couple days spent in the top floor reading room, earphones in, album on, leafing through woodcut prints and learning about alchemy. Alchemy eluded definition and was difficult to understand. Associations of charlatans, deluded chemists, sorcery, occultism, and Satan-worship made it all the more seductive, all the more elusive. Like all things worth pursuing. Like all things Bobby liked. Tracing the enraptured figures with his right index finger, Bobby remembered that Cohen chose that particular woodcut for the cover after Carl Jung used it to describe the ideas of "transference" and "individuation". A union of psychic opposites – a meeting of unconscious and conscious minds.

Bobby twirled the ends of his unkempt beard in a bean-bagged moment of transcendence. It was strange they hadn't thought to discuss this during the trip. (How long ago was it? Well over ten years? Jesus.) But then the CD was pirated, eh. (Did it even have a cover image? Liam kept them in a little wallet.) It seemed more poetic that he found out later, though. Perhaps they were all living in some collective unconscious back then, wailing their way up the Himalayas before their true selves came into consciousness years later through memories and visions of old wise men. Fuck knows. It would be good to read Jung again sometime, he thought. Bobby wenched an index finger under the weighty steel arm of Granda Duthie's vintage wooden record player, delicately placing the needle onto the first track. Warm crackles. Then new promises at dawn. *Is this what he wanted?*

Bobby spent the next half hour or so listening to the

album in full, opting to postpone shaving his shoulders (a Sunday ritual) before the morning walk to Costa. Throughout its cyclical undulations and crackling gravel turns, Bobby thought about music and unconscious memory. About old friends. About Himalayan dirt roads. About Homer and *The Iliad* and *The Odyssey* and oral poetry. About stories and dreams and spiritual quests. About dingy motel rooms. About the oppression of beauty. About lonely ships. And future trips.

Aye. Strange how music could take you backwards and forwards like that. In the gradual untangling of tiredness and dreams, the yellow light of a bright spring morning poured through the flat windows. Bobby roused, and realised he'd probably picked that album since Raj had been texting him more frequently in recent weeks. He'd been asking about Viddy a lot. Making thinly veiled jokes about freaking out at having kids. Talking about Liam's wild idea to meet up on Skye at the start of summer. Something ceremonial was converging, it seemed. The spectral prospects of a journey seemed exciting.

It had been hard for Bobby to stay in touch with any of them over the past few years, partly due to prolonged outbreaks of anxiety, which he took a while to accept or call OCD. No handwashing, no cleanliness, no neatly stacked books; just mental compulsions which varied in their target and content during times of high anxiety, stress, and uncertainty. The worst and most prolonged episode was the oppressive trapping of having to "check" if he was sexually aroused by animals. A walk to Costa might result in him staring at a rear hind or bulbous furry testicles, furiously surveying his thoughts, and spiralling into a panic that he might have felt some sort of sexual attraction. It would surely sound like some ridiculous joke to others, which made the thoughts worse, harder to talk about, more secrecy, which led to more anxiety, which led to more checking, which led to hospitalisation on two occasions, and intensive programmes of CBT that finally helped him acknowledge that not all his thoughts were real nor meaningful. Raj knew bits of what he had been through, but not the truly torturous nature of a mind intent on interrogating itself to the point of destruction and disintegration. Bobby never felt comfortable enough to reveal the content of his compulsions, and Raj probably assumed it was just some kind of general anxiety. It was too hard to be more specific. Too weird. Too shameful.

Bobby took a deep breath and sprung from his brown beanbag. Doing good these days though, eh.

Grateful. Jah Bless.

It would be good to see them all.

Changed days from Delhi capers. But aye.

A lot has happened since.

Aye.

Skye will be good for the soul.

The decision to move hadn't come easy for John and Viddy. The glowing period had passed; her arrival as a farmhand in Ardnamurchan, his boilersuit charm, her woollen tenderness, their double whiskies in the Strontian Hotel, and long summer nights on golden trails peppered with dry, pungent pine needles. It was hard to know where to go and who to

47

be after that summer. But they decided to be together. Viddy wanted away from cities, John from West coast family drama and sectarianism. His family were embroiled in bitter arguments that were at once new and centuries old. Ah, the tranquillity of the Western Highlands.

John's cousin, Neil, had recently passed away without leaving a will. Neil hadn't lived a peaceful of life; abandoned by his father at six, expelled from school at twelve, turning to drink at thirteen, then playing village drunk for the best part of fifty years. At one point he even lived with a sheep, Betsy, in a corrugated iron-roofed croft which John would regularly visit with sympathy gifts of eggs and milk and anything to help Neil sober up. When Viddy first heard about Betsy, she thought it sounded like some kailyard satire cooked up by a poet; only it was a very real, sad situation which John felt partly responsible for, given that his dad, long passed, always looked out for Neil – to the point of leaving a large portion of family land to him, which subsequently decayed.

When Neil's liver finally collapsed, it was up to John to organise the sale of the land, which was to be divided between himself and his two sisters, Fiona and Mary. But John's dad had cut all ties with Mary years ago for marrying a Catholic, leaving John to mediate a sectarian-fuelled sibling feud over lands and inheritance. A blood-and-soil right to belong. The land had no plumbing, no planning permission, and the corrugated iron roof was brown with rust and bad memories. He and Viddy could never live there, and so a quick sale was decided upon, much to the anger of both Fiona and Mary. It would end up in the hands of incomers. Property developers. But John didn't think that mattered too much. He just wanted away from it all. Viddy kept quiet in the tense moments of negotiation. It was none of her business, and she felt like an imposter. God knows what John's dad would have made of her. John did try to reassure her; but the reassurance had intense caveats. Intense ramifications. It was fine. Fine to be brown and Hindu – but not Catholic, apparently, which angered Mary even more. An old wound sliced open. It was probably better for everyone if John and Viddy left to live their life elsewhere.

An old friend from John's agricultural college days was selling a plot on Skye that they could just about scrape a deposit for (with the small cut of his inheritance). But Viddy had reservations. Her welcome in Ardnamurchan had been gentle enough, if warmly paranoid. She understood. At best, she was just another big city incomer, peering in, moving out, maybe coming back to buy a house that wouldn't be lived in for half the year. At worst, she was something else. Something urban, foreign, alien. She remembered reading a pamphlet in the Strontian post office about how the young population of the Highlands and Islands were being forced to leave due to a lack of affordable housing caused by wealthy incomers driving up the market prices. The bullet points were written in black bold ink:

- **The average house price is above £200,000**
- **Once vibrant communities are now desolate due to second homes**
- **No affordable housing is forcing the young population to leave**
- **Our culture is dying**

It was that final point that sent Viddy into a fearful headspin. Fearful anxiety. It was so ambiguous, forceful, nihilistic, almost aggressive. Viddy ambled down the pebbly bank behind the post office and felt something akin to an identity crisis that day. Whose culture was it? How was it dying? Was she part of the problem? It wasn't a bad leaflet. She agreed with it. Agreed with the need for affordable housing; the need to build lives and communities; the need for an active young population; and the need to value indigenous language, music, and art. But that emphasis on culture, heritage, loss. A culture *dying*... It sounded like a blood-and-soil right of belonging and authenticity that she would never have, no matter how hard she tried. She could only live in her own skin. There was no escaping it.

John reminded her not to overthink, or unfairly pre-empt people's reactions; a well-meaning but futile attempt to allay the persistent fears that plagued their pre-move preparations. Fears that led Viddy to reach out in advance to the SCWSC; then later to attend church services, community drives, cattle sales, and primary school coffee mornings before they even had any interest in kids or cows or Christianity. It felt like she overcompensated for the first three years just to prove that she – that someone like her – could contribute to the culture, growth, and future sustainability of the island. It was a pressure John never really felt, never really understood. She forgave him that. It wasn't his fault. How was he to know what it could be like?

She preferred not to dwell when there were things to be getting on with. "Every minute lost in thought was another ten lost in cowshite." "A smile is worth a thousand groans." John was full of little sayings like that. He always made her smile, even though he didn't always see her. But we don't always need to be seen in our entirety to feel love and to love in return. Just getting on with things worked well for Viddy. It's partly why she and Raj didn't work. He was always so bloody intent on reckoning with his own sense of self that he seemed to forget everyone else around him; forget that, for the most part, they actually didn't care, and neither should he.

Viddy didn't have many exes, and she rarely choked on the ashes of old flames. The fling with Raj was easy to get over; only she regretted that it affected their friendship irreversibly, as tends to happen in the aftermath of those temporal flashes of intimacy. It led to the drift. It rarely bothered her, though there were occasional strikes of nostalgia – just enough to indicate something unresolved. Ashes swept under the carpet instead of out the door. There was a moment when she and John were in the red Ford Transit, essentials roped and folded in the back, spirits nervously high and – with no Bluetooth connection – at the emotional helm of whatever songs were on Nevis Radio that morning. When Adele's "Someone Like You" came on, her eyes welled and spilled and welled again in silence as John veered the van up towards Mallaig, humming along obliviously. There's a beautiful fragility to pop music. It's not curated. It plays in background spaces. It plays to the senses and permeates unexpected moments. The melancholic piano provoked an uncontrollable yearning in Viddy that day. The thought of Raj settled down with another girl. They were married now. The time really had flown since that summer haze. She wanted nothing but the best for him. Viddy shuddered and shut her eyes so tight they hurt. She wept again as the melancholic piano rolled along.

Viddy wasn't sure if she was more embarrassed by her silent weeping or its causality – some melodramatic soap opera of a song that had, somehow, permeated her calm sense of self in that moment. Moving was emotional. The sense of motion, movement, wheels rolling ahead, old ghosts left behind.

When Adeepa and Angus yelped their way into their world in the winter of 2016, Viddy had little time to contemplate her past. They nested on the island – made some friends, contributed to the community, and kept their side of the croft clean, so to speak. But none of that even mattered amidst the cycle of feeding, burping, changing, sleeping, kissing, laughing, crying, and bowing to the command of two rabid small mammals. It was a cycle of presence. And for the first time those archaic clichés about parenthood being a grounding experience held more significance. A part of Viddy resented herself for feeling more grounded, and she rarely spoke of it for fear of perpetuating some bullshit ideology about nuclear families and the need for women to reproduce in order to be happy. She had her own way of coming to terms with how she was feeling. Sometimes people strive to forget themselves. Through drugs, music, meditation retreats, whatever works. Being a parent forced Viddy to forget herself. It wasn't necessarily a good thing, nor wilful. It just happened.

Viddy had been fiercely resilient in the wake of change and uncertainty since she was a teenager. It was a quiet, ferocious strength born from the intricacies of faith, ancestry, and immigration; a strength that embodied her very being. She wasn't religious in any conventional sense, having stopped praying with her mother when she was around thirteen. But the step down to her knees, away from prayer, conversely led her back to faith, or at least a version of it that lit a fire within her. Every morning, from the opposite side of the room, she would watch her mother kneel in the quiet corner of their third-floor Tooting council flat.

—Quiet now, Viddy, please. Either join me, or please, quiet.

Her mother would light three sticks of incense, placing one adjacent to each of the sandalwood goddesses, whom Viddy continued to be enraptured by despite her refusal to worship them. By the time Viddy stopped praying, her father's osteoarthritis flamed across his lower back, leaving him bed-ridden for much of her childhood. Yet, with an almost melancholic religiosity, he insisted on reading her *Amar Chitra Katha* comic books every night, summoning her to his bedside with a frail pat on white bedsheets, before charismatically bellowing the trials and tribulations of the multi-coloured, multi-limbed gods and goddesses that became Viddy's superheroes. By the time Viddy stopped praying, then, she was well familiar with Mariamman, Valli, Parvati. They gave her strength in the absence of faith. No longer kneeling, eyes no longer shut, she would watch them every morning in curious serenity, quieting the crunch of her Coco Pops as muted cartoons flashed across the wood-framed television set in the opposite corner. Peering through small clouds of incense smoke, which bellowed across limbs, tridents, cobras, flowers, and fire, she absorbed Mariamman – goddess of rain, curer of disease;

Valli – tribal head huntress and mountain war goddess; and Parvati – goddess of power, nourishment, devotion, and motherhood. At the foot and centre of the three goddesses, there was a photograph of Viddy's grandmother from the early 1900s, black and white tones fighting to conceal the colours of flush leaves, clay pots, and the bangles she evidently still wore to work on the tea plantation.

Viddy's grandparents (on both sides) were "Hill Country Tamils" and derived from a lineage of Tamil Nadu workers recruited by British colonials to labour on tea plantations in the Kandy Plateau, Sri Lanka. Their journey journeyed on through Viddy's mother and her stories. Her songs. Her tears. Their arrival in Sri Lanka by boat from South India; transportation to camps in Matale; and the cold steely prodding of white doctors in white coats and their needles needlessly piercing through brown skin. All in the name of progress. All in the name of civilisation. Many of them died.

Viddy's grandmother, though, was part of a women's trade union movement in the 1940s. They were a radical group that urged liberation from the exploitation of British companies and the caste-based stranglehold they had over tea-plantation workers. Viddy's mother, despite her deep piety, never forgot this. And, consequently, neither did Viddy.

—Religion can be used to oppress as well as liberate, Viddy. Remember that! They used our faith to put us in our place. But come, say your prayers with me, no?

For all the inherited anger against unfair labour; for all the cartilage torn, and swelling across generations, her mother's faith remained – in gods and goddesses and nation-state saviours. After independence, Viddy's grandmother and her comrades in the workers' movements were targeted, weakened, and eventually disenfranchised. Indian Tamils were seen to dilute Sri Lanka; they were impure, didn't belong there. It could never be their home. And so, with masochistic necessity, Viddy's grandmother, now with child in hand, turned back into the arms of Britain. The refuge. The saviour. The good colonist. The provider of a new home. And it worked out, for a while.

Viddy's mother was born into a pre-civil war diaspora that settled in Tooting, London. They were "educated" and forgot the trappings of caste and nation; whilst also forgetting who and what imposed those trappings in the first place. She became a nurse, and nursed the failing health of a husband whose swollen cartilage failed to blight his gratitude towards a new nation, a new home. And they had a daughter, Vidhushei. The possibilities of progress had finally come to bloom.

And in the pungent silences of those smoky teenage mornings in Tooting, Viddy gave birth to a great intensity of light that would shine wherever she walked. The light didn't come from sun, nation, space, or place; but from within herself, within her mother, and within her mother's mother.

It would light the way in the face of dark disease, nourish in times of hunger, and heal in times of pain.

But light, and faith, can be hard to maintain.

Candles flickered in the crackling silence of early evening. Viddy hesitantly thumbed through The Big Skye Scrapbook she and John had started when they arrived. The first page was a Pritt-Sticked copy of the croft deeds, followed by thistles, romantic Polaroids, coffee morning tickets, poems, and the receipt of purchase for three cows, which seemed funny at the time. All that was before the page with two plastic little wristbands, complete with blue biro scrawlings over little white labels: "Adeepa" and "Angus". The following pages changed from pictures and memorabilia relating to themselves to home-printed baby pictures; messy mouths, gummy smiles, and chaotic handprints that spilled over the edges of the page. It was the first time she had looked at the scrapbook since the accident. It didn't teach her anything she didn't know. It was more unsettling than she anticipated, so she clapped it shut and threw it aside. The candle beside her continued to crackle, dance, and flicker as she pulled herself together. It was far easier not to feel. Not to heal.

Viddy cried herself to sleep every night in the first days and weeks following John's death. The twins were too young to know properly. Too young to be damaged. At least, that's what people said in their misplaced attempts to reassure. Nevertheless, Adeepa and Angus reminded her of John at every opportunity in those early days of darkness; crying for "Dada!" at bathtime, before bed, then at breakfast again. She held herself together in front of them and refused to cry in fear of setting them off, so it was the cold black evenings in which she would weep and wail and disintegrate; burying herself under piles of blankets to stop the twins from waking. She even prayed for the first time since she was a child, clamping her eyes shut so tight that they hurt, as tears struggled to seep through the slits of creased eyelids. She prayed for something or someone to take her outside of herself. She prayed for herself to disintegrate and reappear. To live another life away from pain, death, and loss. She even tried reading *Amar Chitra Katha* comic books, which had always been soporific in some nostalgic sense. But there was only pain, then emptiness, then wails, tears, and more sleepless nights.

Then, slowly, over the weeks, then months, then year that followed, the tears began to lessen. She stopped praying. Stopped crying. Stopped feeling. She numbed. She refused to go anywhere that reminded her of him. Anywhere that would make her feel. She wanted him to die. Die. Die completely. Die properly. Just go away.

Viddy slid her palms over her face and listened to the candle crackle. For an intense moment and temporally compressed moment, she imagined the scrapbook burning to a black crisp, smoke seething through charred pages, ashy flakes scattering across the cottage floor.

She shot up.

She needed to finish the list for Freya and get some sleep.

The calamitous unconscious orchestra was wailing its way up the Isle of Skye, and back into her life.

DELHI MOTEL

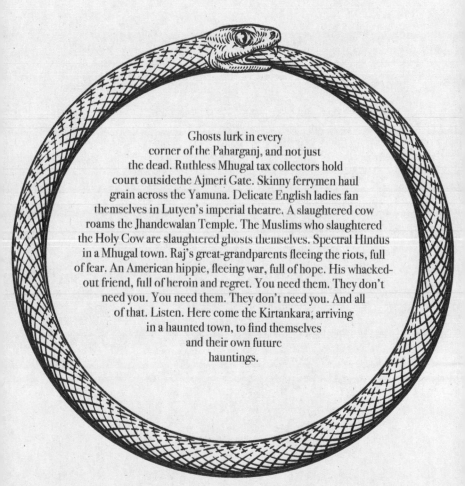

Ghosts lurk in every
corner of the Paharganj, and not just
the dead. Ruthless Mhugal tax collectors hold
court outsidethe Ajmeri Gate. Skinny ferrymen haul
grain across the Yamuna. Delicate English ladies fan
themselves in Lutyen's imperial theatre. A slaughtered cow
roams the Jhandewalan Temple. The Muslims who slaughtered
the Holy Cow are slaughtered ghosts themselves. Spectral Hindus
in a Mhugal town. Raj's great-grandparents fleeing the riots, full
of fear. An American hippie, fleeing war, full of hope. His whacked-
out friend, full of heroin and regret. You need them. They don't
need you. You need them. They don't need you. And all
of that. Listen. Here come the Kirtankara, arriving
in a haunted town, to find themselves
and their own future
hauntings.

O

A few weeks after the collective "fuck it" in The Arlington, they booked flights on a rainy Glasgow summer's day in 2003. Due to different schedules they decided to travel separately, apart from Bobby and Viddy who flew out of Glasgow International together. Liam took advantage of an extra week in Delhi by himself, preceded by a two-day Amsterdam layover, seeing as he was the only one without a part-time job to worry about. Raj joined a week in; Bobby and Viddy arrived a few days after.

Raj's arrival set an early tone of discomfort. Uncanny familiarity in an unfamiliar place. A place he felt entitled to be accepted but clearly wasn't, given his initial welcome. At the arrivals gate, he was pulled aside by two burly Sikh border guards, all moustaches, big bellies, authority, and beige uniforms. They ushered him around the corner to a cork-tiled room that felt yellow and smelled of cigarettes. There were drawing pins on the wall but little else in the way of décor.

—You Indian, sir, no?

—Well, no, I'm from Scotland. I mean, I have a British passport.

—Why you have Punjabi name, sir?

—My dad, he's Punjabi. He moved to Scotland in the '70s. I'm mixed.

The two men gesticulated with their heads and started

61

speaking in what Raj thought was Punjabi. Or maybe Hindi. He'd only ever learned random words:

Doodh
Magaramachchh
Magaramachchh Dundee
Pahalavaa
Chhota Pahalavaan

But the border guards had no interest in talking about milk, crocodiles, Crocodile Dundee or small wrestlers. Raj was clueless and confused by his quarantined state and starting to feel nervous.

—Eh, I could call my dad. Perhaps he could translate some of what you're saying, if it's easier?

They just looked at him stony-faced, possibly offended. Another guard joined them; he was plumper, more jovial, with dark-rimmed spectacles and bad teeth, but of a happy and curious disposition. He seemed charmed by the funnily named, skinny, long-haired hippy before him, but Raj was getting increasingly sweaty, paranoid that his appearance, hair, loose linen, and skin were somehow unacceptable, improper, impure. The plump guard put him at ease, flashing a yellow smile and jiggling his head amiably.

—Okay, sir, please go. Enjoy India, sir.

—Was there an issue with my passport or... ?

—Your name, sir, problem with your name. Rajeev Sabharwal.

—Yes, you see, my dad...

—No matter your dad, Sir. Rajeev Sabharwal in Calcutta escaped murder trial. Killing many women. Running.

—Oh right.

The guards, satisfied that Raj was not the fugitive in their sights, moved their bodies in an unplanned unison of comic gesturing.

—No go to Calcutta!

Raj was relieved but shaken. He never did go to Calcutta.

The hurtling midnight taxi ride towards the Paharganj felt like a montage of stock India footage from some BBC documentary. Or maybe it was the documentary footage that felt like the taxi ride. It was hard to tell. Headlights flashed over the backside of an elephant. Donkeys and amputees peered in windows. Colourful trucks bellowed Bhajans from tinny megaphones. Raj felt shaken, lost; a nervousness took hold of him that he couldn't quite process. He felt spectral, a shadow, head fuzzed by the muggy, noisy evening air. He passed signs, people, and sounds but didn't process any of them as they bent around the car windows.

BANARAS SAREE FACTORY   FANCY FOOT ART

SANGEET MEDITATION CENTRE.   BHANG LASSIS!

Raj drifted his way down a damp alley towards the Shanti Inn, where Liam was waiting in a small twin room lit a dim shade of yellow by an antique-looking lamp. Two Kingfishers and a plate of thali were on a small square table beside the bed, which Liam was lying on before springing up.

—Good to see yi, Raj-ji! How's it gaun? It's mental, eh. Bloody love this place!

Raj smiled and tried to gauge where his friend was at. Liam could be hyper-talkative, all chaos, charisma, and patter; but there was a deeply reflective side to him that often led to quiet spells. It was usually in those moments that he and Raj had the most to say. Calm tangents, where talk of religion, class, Celtic, and ghosts saw them chat long into the night over chai and smoke and mutual awe, mutual attraction.

Raj, still shaken, held both hands either side of his sharp olive cheekbones and smiled at his friend, almond eyes widening. There was no doubt that the pace and sensory fluctuations of Delhi would suit Liam, the gallus wee guy fae the Drum with a taste for madness. He was witty, sharp, cheeky, and possessed a unique manner of self-protection that combined friendliness with unexpected aggression. An inherent edge, or edginess. Haggling would be a challenge he welcomed. Waving his hands, wiggling his head, taking charge of interactions would be effortless. A life of performance would lead to an unexpectedly smooth transition in India, and he'd lap it up with vigour. Incense and Valium and meditation at dusk would usher him into a calmer state in the evenings. It was like a cosmic rhythm which Raj would become simultaneously enamoured and exhausted by. But it was good to be with him again, laugh about a murderous double, make plans for the month ahead.

By the time they finished their Kingfishers, Raj learned that Liam had already sourced charas and found a guy, a solid wee fella called Amrit, who was getting them four bikes – Royal Enfield Bullets. They would ride up to McLeod Ganj, then through the Parvati Valley. Aside Viddy, who buzzed around Glasgow on a Honda 125, the others had never ridden motorbikes. So, the suggestion of vintage bikes on no-rule roads amidst honking taxis, elephants, tuk-tuks, and Himalayan goat herders was a shock to Raj, prompting Liam to check in.

—Yi look a bit shaken, ma man. Y'awrite?

Raj mumbled something about the airport guards and heat and exhaustion. Liam rolled a small joint and reached for the portable CD player and little pamphlet of discs, each tucked inside its own polythene sleeve.

—Yi bring any music, Raj?

—Nah, totally forgot!

Liam continued to leaf through the disc holders, which he thumbed back and forth like blank pages of a book. He tried to light the joint at the same time but there was no gas left in the lighter.

—I'll teach yi an old prison trick, ma man.

Liam ground around the flint wheel so that little particles dispersed onto an empty skin, before the flicker of the flame flared up briefly and the paper crackled into ash. Raj didn't know if Liam had actually been to prison and didn't feel the need to ask as he became entranced by the flaming skin ashing into nothingness before his eyes. Liam exhaled, puffing a smoke ring towards the yellow walls.

—Right, whit yi fancy? A've only got four copied yins. Got a wee fella in the market there doon tae fifty rupees for this. *Best Bhajans,* by Hari Om Sharan. Or there's *Aha Shake Heartbreak*, *Dark Side of the Moon*, and *New Skin for the Old Ceremony*.

Liam, without admitting it, looked to Raj for approval when it came to music, reading, even clothes. Raj was helping him shed old skin.

—Quite ecletic! You managed to get Cohen at a Delhi fleamarket?!
—Aye, ano!
—Stick that oan, son!

The dynamics of Bobby and Viddy's journey a few days later was at a slower tempo than the often frenetic back and forths between Raj and Liam.

Airport pints. People-watching for Bobby. Journaling for Viddy. Hazy jokes and rushed smokes for them both as they waited for a Gatwick transfer. Perched across from the arrival gate, Bobby became transfixed by passengers arriving from Tel Aviv through a revolving door. At one point, a line of Orthodox Jews gracefully strolled through, one after the other, filing across the floor in different shapes and sizes but bound by the striking uniformity of sidecurls, shaved crowns, ankle-skirts, immaculate hats, and tailored coats. The women laughed with one another, little boys twirled at curls, girls patted at plaid headbands, and the men seemed pristine, righteous, intellectual. Bobby caught himself staring and looked away, but some magnetism pulled his gaze back towards them. The aesthetics of the scene, the people, seemed familiar; but he wondered if this was actually his first encounter with Orthodox Jews. It made him wince at his own ignorance, on one hand; and filled him with questions, on the other. He observed how the children looked like miniatures of their parents and wondered about free will and community and belonging.

He thought of himself as a child. His lack of connection to the adults around him. The fairmers who couldn't understand why he was scared of meat. The football coaches who stuck him in goal every Saturday. The teachers who wrongly branded him dyslexic. Then he thought about how sheltered his life had been. How ignorant. How small the sum of his worldly experiences beyond the realms of butteries and battered goods. He felt down. And yet the will, or curiosity, to assume something about others remained strong; but it was offset in this moment by the hard fact that he would probably never know their community – the Orthodox Jews before him. Their hat-makers. Tailors. Barbers. Maybe he would always be ignorant, unless he converted, but that was never going to happen. Then he thought about renunciation. For if the laughing little boy before him was to cut his curls, renounce his family, religion, and home... then would he not always be defined by what he was before? An "ex" Hasidic Jew? Aye, Bobby thought, current status is never defined by what one is, but also what one used to be. Once again, he thought back to himself in primary school. Spotted. Bespectacled. Nervous. Unsporty. Bullied. The only boy in the school canteen who refused Mrs Fowlie's oiled-up kilted sausages (too coorse for the coos). The little boy hadn't left. It defined who he was today. Viddy slapped his arm.

—Bobby! Stop staring!

—Nae staring. Jist thinkin to masel!

It was the first of many thoughts to come over the coming weeks. Bobby and Viddy arrived in Delhi in the afternoon. The air was baking and wet as they stepped out of the aircraft, but it was a far less disorientating experience than Raj's midnight arrival into the dark chaos of night. Bobby was wearing a luminous orange, short-sleeved shirt with green floral flourishes, more fit for Honolulu than the Himalayas. The self-conscious curation of his "tourist look" was completed by the dangling black Minolta 35mm film camera he'd picked up the week before in the West End; part of a holiday-prep whip round the charity shops that had also resulted in the floral shirt, along with ex-military cargo shorts, playing cards, and a Rubik's Cube. It was nice to make an event of the occasion. Viddy appeared effortlessly comfortable and stylish (a hard feat, Bobby thought) in loosely undefined layers of red-brown linen wraps, variously wound around hair, mid-riff and legs to complete her aura of cool.

The flight over had been pleasurable, and time flew fast between conversations about music, in-flight films, Johnnie Walker Black Label miniatures, and the odd moment of reflective journaling (in Viddy's case) and meditative sky-gazing (in Bobby's case). Viddy was occasionally unsure if Bobby's in-flight commentary was purposefully comic or genuinely naïve, but it was funny, harmless, and light from the moment they strapped into their seats.

—Fit?! Viddy, we get our ain wee screen? Like, our ain wee cinema?

—Bobby, you never been on a plane before?

—Nae one with a private wee cinema. At's luxury. Beast, min.

Upon landing, Bobby and Viddy swiftly passed through customs and stumbled outside into the honking frenzy of car horns, concrete crossings, and chaos-conversations. A stream of prospective tuk-tuk and taxi drivers barrelled towards them in cylindrical unison as if they were an egg soon to be fertilised and birthed into the baking hot city. A slender man with an even more slender pencil-moustache reached them first, grabbing at both of their bags, which were safely sheltered between their standing legs.

Scrambling and rambling across them, the slender man spoke quickly and loudly, whilst the other drivers began to trickle back and away from their target, impotent in defeat.

—Sir, let me take your bags and, come come, car is waiting. Where going, sir? Car is very comfortable for you and your wife.

—Well, she's nay actually ma wife. Yi see, we're actually…

Before Bobby could complete a sentence, Viddy intervened, smiling.

—Just go with it, Bobby. It really doesn't matter.

—Ma wife, eh?! Phit will Raj say?!

—What's it got to do with Raj?! Come on, hubby. Let the man take our bags. Chariot awaits, it seems.

Bobby smiled a purse-lipped smile, tightening his eyes and nodding at Viddy as if she had unveiled the secrets of an untranslated Sanskrit holy text, before gently voicing a minor concern about the slender man's continued scrambling and rambling.

—Aye, okay, wifey, okay. Let's ging! But he's nae carrying the bags – here, gies yours.

—Nah, Bobby, just let him. It's easier. He's not going to steal them, for God's sake.

—Steal them?! Nay nay nay. At's nae phit am saying. The man's ma equal, nae ma servant.

—Well, actually, he probably is your servant, Bobby.

—A man's a man, Viddy. Sorry. I mean, a woman's a woman, too. I mean, a man's a man for a that, and a woman's a woman for a that, too. Dah believe in servants. Or kings!

The slender man ceased his rambling and scrambling, apparently perplexed at the couple's converstation. Viddy smiled over a deep sigh simmering within.

—Bobby, it's easier, trust me on this. He'll be more sad not to carry your bag.

—Eh?

—It's his duty.

—It's nae his duty.

—It is. It's his duty, pride, worth.

—A o'er the Earth?

—What?

—Nithin. Ach, fine. Jist dah like bein billy-big baws from the West with his wee Indian servant. Nae richt. Nae richt at a, min.

—It's probably right to him, though.

—Ach, fine, aye. Let's ging! Chariot awaits, wifey.

The slender man slung both rucksacks, along with Bobby's little brown leather satchel, across his back, spine curving upwards, head pointing downwards to support the load – a miraculous and ant-like feat of strength, given the three bags heavily outsized his body. They arrived at the chariot, which transpired to be a faded black and yellow Ambassador taxi-cab with a rusted roof-rack on top. The slender man walked backwards, tiptoeing with elegant and unexpected strength, to slide the three bags simultaneously inside the rectangular roof rack, before swiftly tying it up with frayed blue rope. He turned back to Bobby and Viddy.

—Very safe. No problems. Please, sit inside now. My honour to take you and your wife, sir. Please enjoy.

Whether performed, purely authentic, or pining for a big tip, the slender man's powerful proclamations of honour jolted them into the taxi with a sense of purpose. Bobby nodded knowingly at Viddy, whilst she sat back slowly into the torn leather seats and took out a pen and pocket-moleskin as the Ambassador honked and harried its way out of the busy airport car park. As the car creaked to an abrupt stop shortly after exiting, Viddy looked past three rows of traffic-jammed, honking cars to gaze upon a bony but strikingly beautiful elderly woman sitting on the road-side in rags. Matted grey hair, head facing down towards the dirt, and one twiggy brown arm raised with two fingers pressed together. The slender man managed to manoeu-vre through the car-chaos and the beautiful twiggy woman receded into the distance, into the dirt, and into the dust. Viddy was stoic, serious, and spoke quietly in a way that was barely audible above the high-pitched outside chaos and the low, rumbling of the Ambassador engine.

—Some people think it's a divine choice. People suffer-ing like that.

—Yi mean caste? Aye, da get it.

—Oh, I get it. Purity. Pollution. Power. Politics. I get it. It's no different to racism.

—Aye. But is it nae religious?

—It is. Or maybe it was. Some story about Brahma's body. Like, how his feet were more impure than his fingers or mouth or head, just like the comic books say to every innocent Hindu child. Fuckin' indoctrination. But it's really about power. And I don't know if there's anything anyone can do about it.

—Aye. Nithing holy about that, eh.

—Religion can be used to oppress as well as liberate, I suppose.

—Aye. Aye.

Placing her notebook aside, Viddy leaned further back into the fragmented foam protruding from the ripped leather headrest. She thought about her mother, and grandmother, and gods and goddesses, and praying, and displacement, and home, and homelessness. She thought about the slender man's pride. And whether pandering to his pride was the same as bowing to entitled elites. She thought about the helplessness of it all. It's why there was never any point in praying.

Bobby, perceptive to his friend's feelings, broke her reverie gently, without abrasive intrusion.

—Yi alright, wifey?

—Yeh. Bit tired. But glad to be here. It's exciting, y'know? New smells, new people, new thoughts.

—Aye. Yi hungry?

—I can wait. I'm sure Raj and Liam have plans of some sort, knowing them.

—Aye. Weel. Here's a pack o Scumpy Fries fur now.

—Thought you were going veggie on this trip?

—I am. Scumpy Fries are nae sentient, ken.

Bobby and Viddy arrived at the motel as dusk began to darken, opening the twin-bedroomed door to Raj and Liam, hugs and incense and smoke and Leonard Cohen.

They laughed and listened and talked.

It became a nightly ritual.

A ceremony.

Simultaneously ambiguous and binding.

The menorah, cross, or crescent used to make visible some palpable and unseen collective spirit felt in the multitude as well as the individual.

And the music played on into the night, every night.

With three days to spare in Delhi while Amrit promised to super-fix and polish-kindly the Royal Enfields, the four friends decided to take in some sights. One morning they woke in ceremonial haze to catch a dark clanging minibus in the direction of the Red Fort to watch the sun rise. Each of them took a separate window seat, fatigued and slouching, heads pattering against lukewarm glass as the city began to sing itself awake in the slow morning light. Holiness wailed from megaphone speakers; engines rumbled; railroads drummed; horns parped; throats gargled; and the clink of milk bottles chimed with the clank of hammers on anvil.

The rhythmic bus ride to the Red Fort must have been around fifteen minutes but felt suspended in some thought-motion cycle of elasticity. This may well have been due to the previous night's (was it still night?) ceremony, or the Carlos Vallies before bed – but either way it was a rare quiet space with which to think through their body's presence in a place their minds had long imagined, all in different ways.

Liam, more so than the others, bought into the mythology of where he might find himself. He was not wholly naïve. He'd read *Karma Cola.* He knew about the postcolonial commodification of tourism. Worn tales of glaikit hippies looking for meaning, wisdom, tantric sex, and cheap drugs in all the wrong places with all the wrong gurus. But it was *still* intoxicating. Embarrassingly seductive. And so he continued to read about Schopenhauer, Emerson, and Madame Blavatsky finding light in *The Upanishads*. About medieval oriental epiphanies during the crusades. About Orlovsky and Ginsberg and Ram Dass rambling around Varanasi smoking oily hashish with Bengali poets. It was hard not to be intoxicated. Hard not to be affected by all those imaginings, all those epiphanies. Even if they were dreamt, and dreamt again, they seemed no less real to him.

Raj's imagined relationship to India was equally as strong, but fraught by the fact that it represented a fragile connection to his father. Watching the streets wriggle to life through the lens of a blurry bus window, Raj grappled, as he did throughout the trip, with his sense of disconnection to place, people, and how their pasts were also his pasts. He wanted to belong. But knew nobody. He wanted to feel whole. But was fragmented. His connections were imagined, not real. His family had long lost touch. Nothing left but fragments of language, pigments of skin. Viddy tried to convince Raj that his kinship could be real *and* imagined. Walking meditatively around the Red Fort, they spoke quietly in the bare honesty of morning.

—Can't process it, Vid. I feel something here. Like it's part of me. But I might just be imagining it, y'know?

—And?

—Dunno. Just makes me feel lost. It's different for you. You've still got loadsa family in Sri Lanka. Y'even look Sri Lankan, fucksake!

—Christ, Raj, stop. If this place feels part of you, embrace it. It's still you. And it's real. No, actually, it's not even real.

—Eh?

—Look where we are. The Red Fort. It's not even Indian.

Viddy eased Raj's confusion, gesticulating with her notebook in the red humid sun.

She spoke with a circular knowledge that stretched backwards through books and forwards through familial experience. The hierarchies of past and personhood seemed to collapse into one for a moment as Raj looked at her with love and want while she untangled the undefined ancestral knots inside himself. She spoke of the Mughal and Maurya Empires. Mathematicians. Astronomers. Scientists. Kings and gods and queens and goddesses. Jains and Sufis and Buddhists. The sheer fallacy of a unified state. The sheer fallacy of a unified religion. The sheer fallacy of a unified self. The dangerous toxicity of purity, self-determination, cohesion. The oppression of belonging.

Viddy took a deep breath and flicked through to the back pages of her notebook, pointing to a boldly scrawled quotation which she read aloud.

—"Thou art the ruler of the minds of all people."

—Meaning?

—I guess it's yours to imagine. Or just let go a little. Look at Liam, he's having no trouble!

They glanced over to the Red Fort gardens where Liam was sitting cross-legged, having his face painted by a slender bearded sadhu; both seemingly humming together in some impromptu transcendental dawn song. Raj let out a quiet laugh.

—Fucksake!

—It's cool though. He's got such enthusiasm – the way he embraces a place he's only ever imagined. There's something in that.

—Aye, maybe.

Raj eased into the idea, but remained uncomfortable, fraught. Surely those relationships of the mind were detached from the harsh realities of actual experience. The same detachment that led to glaikit hippies on the hunt for cheap heroin, or lycra-clad yoginis looking to find the light in Goa. The unholiness of Hinduvata, the corrupt dynasticism, the anglophone oppression, and the BJP didn't matter a bean when your thoughts were absorbed by a chai latte after yoga practice with some bearded medicine man horny for the evening ahead. All those imagined relationships were damaging to the reality of people's lives. Raj was different. He had an *actual* connection, a *deeper* understanding. So why was he forced to imagine? Maybe they were all one and the same. It was hard to know how to be.

Just prior to the trip, Raj and Liam were reading Walter Scott for an English module called "Romantic Nationalisms". It led to several drunken chats about belonging and Scotland and constructed identities over after-class pints. Sometimes their lecturers even came along, quietly waltzing into the Chip like caricatures, replete with brogues, waistcoats, and leather satchels. Raj remembered one evening, in particular, where they had been talking about "roots tourism" in the Highlands. One of the historians, typically cock-sure and full of beer and facts and empiricism, was describing the phenomenon of diasporic descendants of the Scottish Highlands returning to their "homeland" to find connection and belonging in the landscape, despite not knowing anyone there, nor much about the reality of life beyond kilts and whisky and cute phrases. One theory for this apparent pining for an authentic homeland was because Scots, according to the stout and salivating historian, had settled in various British colonies where dispossessed indigenous peoples appeared to impinge upon the newcomers' capacity to belong. So, pilgrimages from the likes of Canada and New Zealand to the Scottish Highlands became quests to belong through landscape, myths, and distant genealogical clan connections that enabled their own "indigeneity"; or their own need to find an authentic and unproblematic sense of belonging that had become impossible in their new homelands.

Raj remembered scoffing at the idea. He'd cringed during brief encounters with Americans, usually in Edinburgh, in full tartan garb and proudly proclaiming heritage and haggis and ancestors in Culloden. It seemed desperate. Comical. What about all the other heritages? They just wanted to privilege their white Scottish Highlander one through myth, imagination, and Walter Scott's clan histories, which bore little resemblance to actual historical fact. The connection between blood and soil was illusory and made Raj shudder. Yet here he was, pondering his ancestors around the Red Fort, in some unspoken quest for a more authentic sense of belonging. Perhaps blood and soil was the problem. We could all use our imaginations more.

While Liam played with facepaints and Viddy entertained Raj's introspections, Bobby curved himself into the repetitive arcs of a sandstone Mhugal wall, observing, as he often did, the others. On the flight over, two plastic bottles of mini-JD and a packet of peanuts down, he had asked Viddy if it might be strange for Raj to be in an "ancestral homeland". He knew Raj's hang-ups, probably better than anyone. To Bobby, comfortably rooted in his own Aberdeenshire soil, it was all a matter of colonial entanglements. Raj's disquiet was one that arose from being born privileged in the seat of empire. Even worse, being born the son of a father who refused to acknowledge the dispossession of Indian peoples and cultures. Railways, roads, education. He even got a scholarship to study in the UK and rise above the circumstances his caste would typically allow for. Raj was too much of a dissident to acknowledge the complexities of that colonial mindset. Which is why Bobby thought of it as an Oedipal struggle against colonialism which led to disquiet, searching, even Raj's peculiar own brand of roots tourism.

Bobby lit a cigarette – a small green cylindrical wrap, picked up in the Paharganj for fifteen rupees and resembling a tightly rolled autumn leaf, skin overlapping skin. It tasted weak and bitter. Perhaps he was lucky to be so rooted in the songs and soil of the North-East. Perhaps he would look into it more when he got back.

A long way to come to think about where you're from.

Maybe that was India.

Perhaps there *was* truth in imagining.

LOVER LOVER LOVER

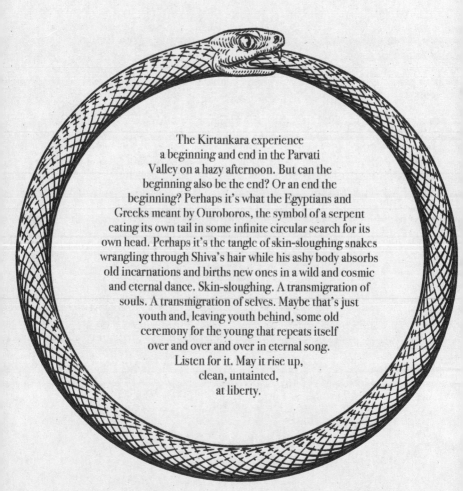

The Kirtankara experience
a beginning and end in the Parvati
Valley on a hazy afternoon. But can the
beginning also be the end? Or an end the
beginning? Perhaps it's what the Egyptians and
Greeks meant by Ouroboros, the symbol of a serpent
eating its own tail in some infinite circular search for its
own head. Perhaps it's the tangle of skin-sloughing snakes
wrangling through Shiva's hair while his ashy body absorbs
old incarnations and births new ones in a wild and cosmic
and eternal dance. Skin-sloughing. A transmigration of
souls. A transmigration of selves. Maybe that's just
youth and, leaving youth behind, some old
ceremony for the young that repeats itself
over and over and over in eternal song.
Listen for it. May it rise up,
clean, untainted,
at liberty.

Bobby felt his breath in harmony with every pull and push of the harmonium bellows. Two droning bass notes echoed down river, up the rockface, and into the bodies of Raj, Liam, Viddy, and the four Shaivites. One of them droned a ghostly echo, calling for a response, *Ommmmmmmm Nava Shiviyah, Ommmmmmm Nava Shiviyah, Hari Om Nava Shiviyah.* The others beat tabla and began to dip and dance and circle around the smoke and fire. Particles of ash blended with bodies, semi-naked, chalked grey, jet-black hair flowing up and around the air like the dark estuaries of some sacred river. The tabla beat faster, Bobby breathed quicker. Lungs and body and bellows followed suit. The droning vibrations grew louder, and the ghosts began to clap, to make their presence known in the universe. Liam, Raj, and Viddy danced wild in cosmic song. Clapping. Chanting. Circling the ash clouds. Entranced. Happy. Young. Liberated from themselves.

The cosmic dance with spectral Shaivites made the tumultuous motorcycle trip from Delhi up to the Parvati Valley worthwhile. It had tested them all – in stamina, friendship and ill-equipped motorcycling knowledge. Little squabbles had broken out before they even left. Liam liked to control things: the bikes, where to go, what to take, what was safe to eat. He was marginally older than the others by four years, being a latecomer to university life, and possessed, amidst all his exploratory open-mindedness and desire for learning, a well-founded belief that he had more life experience, harder life experience, than the others. The type of experience that might be needed when four motley friends with little motorcycling knowledge ride up to the Himalayas. Bobby, probably the least strung out of the four, was intent on having fun, but having fun meant buying a harmonium. Liam wasn't entirely sure what a harmonium even was but had pretty strong reservations about it.

—How tha fuck yi gonna carry a harmonium on a motor-bike? Yer gonnae kill yersel, ya madman.

—Aye, you can get wee harmoniums, like.

—Fucksake, man.

Raj and Viddy convinced Liam it would be fine, that it would be fun to have music when camping, and Raj had brought along a travel guitar anyway. A couple of days before they left Delhi, the four of them wound up in a small cove of a shop at Janpath Market called Vijay's Harmonium Emporium and Tropical Fish Shop. The sidewalls of the room were laden with makeshift palette shelves with goldfish swimming in a selection of algae-green globes. They didn't look too tropical. The back of the room was a wall of stacked harmoniums, all different shapes, sizes, colours; some of them plain and some beautifully ornate. Ivory. Marble. Plastic. Greens. Gold. Purple. Bobby explained he was looking for a small and relatively inexpensive one, ideally something that he could strap to his back.

—Yes, my friend, understand. You travelling, small harmonium. Where you from?

—Scotland.

—Ah, bagpipes, sir! Indian bagpipes very good, %100 quality. No bagpipes here. Two types of harmonium, different styles. Delhi harmonium or Kolkata harmonium? Kolkata much better, my friend. Quality %100. Engineering %100.

As soon as he said it Raj jumped in, seemingly panicked.

—Don't get a Calcutta harmonium, Bobby.

—Eh? Why yi being weird?

Raj couldn't really explain it, but after just a week in Delhi he seemed to have tuned into signs and signifiers that might have meant something or nothing at all. But he wasn't taking any chances. He began to listen more closely, as they all came to do, as the universe unfolded itself.

After much haggling and head gesturing, Bobby decided that a purple Delhi harmonium was best anyway. Smaller, more compact, %100 quality Punjabi reeds vertically arranged, twenty-five keys, and a portable pine box with backstraps and flamboyant gold string decor. Ideal for travelling. They left the shop, drank chai, and spent the rest of the morning at Janpath, picking up last-minute supplies for the road. Mango-flavoured bidi's, mathri, a mosquito net, a beige silk wrap for Viddy's hair, a black silk wrap for Raj's hair, a dog-eared copy of *Zen & The Art of Motorcycle Maintenance* for Liam, and a bottle of "Happy Highlander Blended Whisky" for them all.

Between then and reaching the Parvati Valley, something congealed among them that took years to fade, if it ever did. Fights, love, crashes, and youthful hope consolidated into that rare life moment of being in the right place, with the right people, at the right time. Though it didn't always feel like it. The trip started with Bobby crashing into a goat, sending it and a table of fresh mangos rolling into the side of the road, to much uproar and chaos. It seemed to happen in slow motion – and it partly did, given that he was travelling at about 5mph. Bobby later believed some divine providence to be at work that day, as he lay on the road like a tortoise, stubby limbs in the air, pine harmonium shell under his back, cracked, but breaking his fall.

Then there was the incident with the widos. Bobby's bike was sputtering fluid, sounding sick, and so they stopped for help in Joginder Nagar. A crowd gathered as a skinny, frail-looking man who called himself Joe set to work with rusty tools, and the four of them took shelter from the baking heat under the umbrella of a chai stall. Three men approached, two in black bandanas, one in a red baseball cap, smiling, but sinister. The one with the baseball cap had a rifle slung over his shoulder. He did the talking.

—Where you go, friends?

Liam took charge, he always did if he sensed a threat, much to the annoyance of Viddy. Liam and Bobby were happy to sit quietly, heads bowed.

—Up the Parvati Valley, ma man.

Liam smiled confidently, but the others saw through his performance. He was nervous. On edge and tetchy under the skin as the man replied.

—Parvati Valley, okay okay. We pay for your chai. Come with us to Jammu. Many nice things there.

—Naw, yer alright, ma man, save yer money! We'll be on the road soon. Going north.

—Okay okay. You pay for our chai then, no?

Liam laughed, this time audibly nervous, forcing the pronounciation of his words and vowels with a wavering voice, wide eyes.

—Naw naw, brother. You pay for your chai, we pay for ours, and we'll hit the road, eh?

—No chai? So, we not your friends, uh?

—We're all friends, brother, but let's buy our own chai, eh.

The man with the rifle was stout, with a cauliflower nose and scar on his left cheek. He looked at his friends and started laughing. Liam whispered fast, covertly to Raj.

—These bawbags-are-on-the-bam-up-eh.

Liam tried to look cool; Bobby appeared frozen in Lotus Pose, head bowed and aviators hiding his fear; Viddy sat calmly, glaring at the men with a vicious smile. The man with the rifle smiled at her.

—Who's the darling? How much she cost? Very nice. Does nice things for you, no? Three lovers, poom poom!

The men laughed louder, and the cauliflower nose snorted out some kind of pollen. Liam's mouth twitched. Raj felt hurt for his friend. Viddy braved a smile as she walked towards the man.

—Yeh! Three lovers, Baba-ji – more expensive than you could ever afford.

The men snorted. Liam was right, they were on the bam up, but they also had a gun.

Viddy smiled through the hurt, as she had done countless times before. Throughout the trip, she'd noticed the way people were looking at her. Her dark skin. The company of two "Westerners", or maybe three, seeing as Raj kept being mistaken for Israeli. And there was no escape from the signs – actual signs – on billboards, beauty shops, and Bollywood posters. Roadside flickers at the edge of her helmet, peripheral flashes on repeat.

FAIR & LOVELY. POND'S WHITE BEAUTY. ENAMI
FAIR & HANDSOME.

It wasn't the first time she'd felt determined by her complexion, but it was magnified here, and it felt oppressive to be trapped in her own skin with no way of sloughing everything that came with it. Cauliflower nose persisted.

—So, friends, Jammu with us, yes?

The situation was getting increasingly unsettling, and Liam was starting to think it might be more than just ill-placed patter. Something like this would never bother him back home. He knew how to perform, owned the stage, and had done since he was a wee boy. When Liam was five, a plump older boy with a red mushroom haircut asked him to pick up a thick slimy slug and hide it in one of the girls' shoes whilst they were skipping and rhyming the playtime away. Mushroom-heid had got wind from James that Liam had a deep fear of slugs, which he did – he physically shook at the thought of them. But acutely aware of the social significance of the situation in terms of performance and hierarchy, Liam didn't just pick up the slug, but scurried around to find five more in the soily edges of a flowerbed, supressing his shaking fear as he copped them up. It was a heavy burden to act differently to the way he felt, but it was worth it. Rather than place it in a girl's shoe, he snuck up behind mushroom-heid and smeared the slugs down his neck, thereby inaugurating "Sluggy Mushroom-heid", who never lived it down, and wee Liam the madman, who never let his status slip again.

And so, an innocent wee boy was born into a world of performativity. A world that saw him rise above ranks. A world that sometimes spiralled into violence. A world that, as he got older, made him simultaneously invincible and nauseous. It was hard to maintain, partly because he was so aware of it as an *act*. Some men actually believe it. They get seduced by the supposed authenticity of historically strong masculine ideals, causing them to spiral into violence and vulnerability if they can't match up, can't man up. But it was the very performativity of it all that crushed Liam. A double-bind of a way of being, which on one hand granted him societal status and, on the other, tore at his inner ideals. Only, in this new context, he was unsure of his lines. This was a different stage. A different world.

Thankfully for Liam, he didn't have to put new lines to the test, as he caught sight of Joe, whose cream lungi were now smeared in oil stains. Creeping behind the men, Joe threw a glare of caution and repeatedly pointed to the bikes with his thumbs up. With a skinny thrust of his chapped, bony leg, Joe kick-started the engine for Bobby, which caused the men to turn around as the others swiftly hopped past them and onto their bikes, riding off after Liam slapped a pile of notes into Joe's hands. They could still hear the men chortling as they changed gears, clunking second into third, off up the dirt road, rumbling onwards. Bobby led the way, pulled the throttle hard, causing his legs to clamp around the fuel tank in fear of road goats. Viddy and Raj followed, and Liam rode at the back at a slower pace, looking over his shoulder cautiously at every turn.

The guidebooks and travel demi-gods (those dreadlocked, loose-linen, yellow-toothed, hemp-smelling clones kicking about hostels) had all said that McLeod Ganj would feel unlike anywhere else in North India. After the widos at Joginder Nagar, any place of relative peace and cool was welcome; but all expectations were surpassed the moment the four of them breezed into the clean, floral air of Dhara-masala. They arrived at a dusty square plaza next to a line of taxis and buses, gingerly yanking their limbs off bikes to feel the cool air on their hot, clammy skin. It wasn't rain-ing but it felt and smelt like it should be; the air was flush with a pungent, planty moisture, and puddles from rains past dozed like country pools across the plaza. There was no shortage of bright signs fading into the dusky light.

JIMMY'S ITALIAN PIZZA PLACE

BEST COACH TRAVEL INDIA

MANGO BANG LASSI BONANZA

Yet despite the apparent tourism, there remained an unexpected stillness to the place. By this point, they had become accustomed to fuel stops and first arrivals being a flurry of chaos; chai wallahs, scruffy chickens, turbaned hoteliers, pocket-pulling children, and the constant clam-our of engines, animals, and haggles. But here, amidst the quiet patter of a few travellers and some luminously bald monks, there was an immediate air of tranquillity. Raj even heard the distant echo of someone playing scales on a flute – the simple and monotonous practice of someone who he would never meet.

The dusty square plaza was the small heart of McLeod Ganj, swirling into various narrow arteries that ascended the mountainous terrain shading the village. On the advice of a frail old man, all wrinkles and cheekbones and flaming red hair, the four of them ambled up a sharp gradient towards Samir's Guesthouse.

The absence of haggling and harrying felt strangely disconcerting after days of performing various version of themselves: too tired to talk, stuck-up, shy, intimidating, intimidated, frustrated, ignorant, arrogant. The attention had affected them all differently. Collectively, they explained it away in the murky peace of dingy guesthouse rooms as something all tourists face; and they were, perhaps, a particularly motley bunch of friends. Individually, it was more complex.

Liam lapped up the endless possibilities for good patter, best equipped as he was with witty quips, and offering his usual token of a cigarette to strangers to break down any sense of hierarchy. It was a simple act, but a masterful gesture, which Raj observed in admiration. Liam had consequently been met with great hospitality wherever he roamed. He'd been invited to join a circus, play a minor Bollywood part, sell opium, and become a corporate advocate for India's burgeoning plastics industry. And that was all in the space of a single train ride.

For Raj, it was harder. Creepings of paranoia and some unresolved trauma blighted his ability to discriminate between the types of attention he was receiving. Perhaps others found him as hard to place as he did himself. Perhaps they saw something Indian in him. Or not. Then there was the airport border guards; the Sikh waiter in Delhi who said he had "Punjabi eyebrows"; the puzzled looks when hostel staff opened his passport; and, most commonly, the Hebrew greetings from fellow travellers. Rather than helping him to trace a sense of self and heritage, the trip was, on the contrary, splintering Raj, forcing him to over-think how others saw him, and who he should be.

This absence of coherence reminded him of when he was younger, just after his parents divorced. There was a period where his dad, not long after moving to Birming-ham, would come to visit Raj in Glasgow, or sometimes Newcastle, and the two of them would stay in Travelodges; awkwardly catching up, eating Brewers Fayre cheeseburg-ers, trying to ignore each other's snoring in a cramped twin bedroom. On one occasion, Raj overheard a couple of burly, bald, polo-shirted guys with Geordie accents at the bar chatting and nodding in the direction of them.

—Them lads together, like?

—At's disgoostin, man.

—Flippin pervert!

The looks, whispers, and reactions to Raj – then skinny, long hair, pale to olive season-dependent complexion – and his dad – portly, dark brown skin, Punjabi brows – set in an underlying paranoia about how others saw him in different moments, with different people. It was an internal tension that was heightened in India, leading to little outbreaks of nervous anxiety.

If Raj was overly observant of strangers, Bobby's sto-icism and knowing caution reigned his three companions into balance. Less concerned with how others saw him, Bobby's omniscient eyes, circled behind thick lenses, saw it all. Raj's insecurities, Viddy's melancholic sensitivities, and Liam's hyper-patter friendships. He tempered them into union when they needed it most. And so, on Bobby's gentle command, they headed for the winding, rocky path up towards Samir's Guesthouse, after Liam had found out what kind of hair dye the frail old man used to attain his fringe of glowing fire.

They arrived in the guesthouse reception to find Samir cross-legged in front of a square little television on the floor with an inbuilt catflap-like compartment for VHS tapes. The rectangular room was decorated with squint pictures of romantic hill station tea parties and posters of Queen Elizabeth, set off by tin-pot tiffany lamps and a large reddish Kashan rug, which Samir was sitting on. There were no tables nor furniture. The proprietor sat sipping from a small china teacup and saucer while watching tense points played out at the 1992 Wimbledon men's final. Samir, skinny and elegant in a loose cotton button-down shirt, jet-black trousers, and even blacker oiled hair, flicked his wrist around in the air to welcome the visitors with a palmy gesture as he heard the bell on the door chime ambiently.

—Welcome, friends. Wimbledon, no? 1992 final. Very good.

The VHS taping was blurry. White streaks wobbled across the face of a skinny Goran Ivanišević as he paced up and down in frustration as Agassi – swagger, cap, and peroxide locks – gained momentum in the set. For a good three minutes or so, Samir continued to watch the points play out as the four of them stood watching him watch Wimbledon 1992, backpacks still strapped on and pulling at their shoulders. After a break in play between games, the score flashed up in a large, yellow, embossed font. Liam picked his moment carefully.

—Samir, ma man, how's it gaun? I remember Agassi and all! Watched this when I wiz a wee guy. Class, so he was.

Samir turned to face them for the first time, revealing his beautifully smooth light brown skin and angular features offset by thick bundles of black hair.

—Agassi. Wears a wig, no?

—Eh, ah'm no sure, Samir. Think that wiz his actual hair. '90s, y'know!

—No no. Wig.

—Mibbe, Samir, aye!

—But wig, no wig – no problem! Shanti shanti!

—Shanti shanti, ma man!

—Wig-no-wig-no-problem! Shanti shanti!

—Yer a madman, Samir!

In some blend of relief and tiredness and tenderness from the long day, the four of them laughed, then giggled again, and began to shanti shanti along with Samir, for whom nothing was a problem, it seemed, not even Andre Agassi's wig at the 1992 men's Wimbledon final. After proudly showcasing the Edwardian boardings – more Kashan carpets, tinpot Tiffanies, and pictures of the Queen, to Liam's great amusement and irk – Samir led them halfway down a sloping path at the back of the guesthouse, which looked over a flush green tapestry of tea gardens, conifers, and pines peppered with the slow-motion movements of maroon-robed monks in hemp summer robes and stubble heads. They appeared to be levitating around the greenery.

With the promise of some lovely lovely evening tea and shanti shanti music, Samir continued down a wooded walkway which pierced through the flush greenery towards a little bamboo shack decorated with colourful cloth prayer flags. Samir palmed apart the bamboo partition at the front of the hut, and they were greeted warmly by what, at first sight, seemed to be a band. There was a large Belgian named Jed, trumpet strewn lazily across his torso. Beside him sat a beautifully androgynous Tibetan with a guitar who introduced himself as Flash, and finally a tall, lean, bearded man at the back of the room named Ashoke who wore horn-rimmed spectacles and a Himachali cap.

The little shack was strewn with strawmats, steaming tin teapots, porcelain cups, paisley pillows, and musical instruments of various kinds, including guitars, bamboo flutes, tabla, and ornate, wooden, stringed objects that resembled violins. There were two large pictures on the wall which immediately struck Raj. One was a photograph of a gaunt old man in a suit, possibly Indian, possibly not, sitting elegantly on a delicately carved chair next to a stack of library books. A man of learning, of some significance, it seemed. Next to that photograph there was a larger, frayed tapestry of a grey-haired man being held aloft on a large paisley pattern cushion, brandishing some kind of wand, much to the veneration of the wise, bearded Sikh men who all sat below him. It looked like there were four winged angels hovering around his head. Raj wondered if the protagonist in each picture was the same person, but he couldn't tell.

After a round of pungent tea had been poured and consumed with the passing of a chillum, Viddy gracefully sprang from the bamboo floormat she was sitting on to say she was heading back to the guesthouse. It had been a long day. Bobby followed, shortly after. It *had* been a long day, but he was wondering if Viddy was leaving due to fatigue, or feeling too stoned, or perhaps she just wanted to be alone and free from paternalistic concerns which would surely get patronising. He was tired anyway, so he made for the gently sloping wooded path back to the guest-house. Ambling up the square steps, which had been dug from mud and framed in timber, Bobby glanced up to find Viddy standing transfixed in the centre of one of them. She was staring at a circle of glowing monks sat meditating on the forest floor a few hundred yards to her left. They were barely visible but beautiful in the green and black darkening of the night. Bobby panted up towards Viddy and was out of breath by the time he stood next to her in the centre of the square step. Finally catching enough wind to pech out a couple of words, he turned towards her.

—Y'arite, Vids?

—Yeh. Do you think they are happy? They look sombre.

—Probably mair happy than us. Less trappings, onyway.

—Yeh. Renunciation, though. Bet inner peace comes at a high cost.

—Fur the greater good though, eh?

—Yeh. Maybe.

The two of them stood for a few more seconds that seemed to stretch and elongate into minutes. Viddy thought about her dad reading *Ashoka* to her. Peace over blood at the cost of renouncing a son, a daughter, a wife. No family. Ascetic living for better giving. Was it worth it? Probably. All for the Dharma. All for the Dhamma. And now that wheel of his was bang in the middle of a flag flown to flout Hindu nationalism. Was it worth it? Viddy stretched her back, pelvis thrusting forwards and head thrown backwards. Bobby sensed her fatigue.

—Sure yer 'arite?

—Yeh. Fine. I don't think I'll ever know that life. Or pretend to understand it.

—Aye. Wiz thinking the same aboot Orthodox Jews afore.

—Orthodox Jews?

—Disnae matter. Bedtime?

The two of them trapsed up the remainder of the muddy, wood-framed stairs to the guesthouse, where they fell into an Edwardian slumber within minutes.

Back in the shack, another round of pungent tea was poured and the chillum passed round again. Jed pressed the trumpet mouthpiece to his lips and effortlessly exhaled a rising melody; Flash fingerpicked along, spectral harmonics here and there; while Ashoke, Liam, and Samir fell into a long and deep conversation about the history of Mcleod Ganj, the colonial era, Orientalism, Tibet, the Dalai Lama, caste, and tea and chillums and more tea and chillums and some pamphlet about particles and stars and the universe unfolding itself.

Reclining backwards, horizontal on his bamboo mat, Raj heard what he thought was light rainfall patter against the tinshack roof, chattering like falling teeth from above. Erratic drips, rising melodies, raised hands, oriental scholars, widos, Wimbledon, and wigs. And then mist appeared, or maybe smoke, rising from the earth or falling from the sky.

He thought he might be dreaming.

It was impossible to tell.

Rattly snares of phlegm roused Raj from his deep sleep. He was back in the guesthouse, legs coiled with Viddy's on one of the twin beds in the large square Kashan-carpeted room.

The messy strewn sheets adjacent meant that Bobby and Liam had likely left for a misty morning chai, or just needed to escape each other's odours outside the shared room sleeping arrangements. Things could get very pungent, very quickly. Viddy gently pleated strands of Raj's wiry, humid hair. The left side of his head fell back against her propped-up torso as she gazed contently out of the small, square, bamboo-framed window. Outside, a frail skeleton of a man faded in and out of view. Offsetting the frailty was a thick silhouette of beard and prominent nose which both rippled amidst sporadic grunts and bodily gunk. Beyond the triumphant nostrils, intricate patterns of colourless lines appeared in the hemp mist; a morning mountainscape yet to be realised. Viddy braided strand over strand, whispering gently as Raj roused further.

—You slept deep. Like a baby.

—Yeh. Yeh, I did.

—Although you did seem pretty high when you came to bed.

—Eh, aye. I suppose. That mad Samir, man. You sleep okay?

—Yeh. Dreams of white horses.

—That's poetic.

Raj rustled the silky brown embroidered sheets to one side, grabbing hold of his Shiva pendant while pulling back his shoulders to ease the tension in his shoulders. Upright and hazy, twisting his olive torso, he turned back to Viddy.

—It feels like a special place here, eh?

—It's different to the last few days, that's for sure. Feels calmer.

—I'm so glad you're here, Viddy. You really get me. You know that right?

Viddy glanced back out the window, where gunky grunts continued to break the misty morning silence, before uneasily turning back towards Raj. It felt like he wanted to hear something profound, but Viddy didn't concede.

—We should go find Bobby and Liam. What are we doing today, anyway?

Raj bowed in prayer-like position, placing his head back on the bed, peeking upwards.

—Don't you want to stay here a little longer with me? It feels special.

Viddy smiled and rubbed his back whilst simultaneously rising out of the bed and gathering her clothes together in a call to action.

—You're right, it is a special place. Let's go see it. To the mountains we go!

Raj coiled his head back towards the bed, faced down for a moment, then rose up gingerly and got dressed.

Clouds of bidi smoke engulfed the small corner of the chai shop Bobby and Liam were squatting in as they watched the mountains come to colour and life. Viddy rustled through the tassled entrance, dipping her head below colourful bunting, and draped herself next to Bobby and Liam. Their respective linen trousers formed a kind of dreamwork under the chai table. Raj sleepily followed in after Viddy, turning to Bobby for a light.

—Got a light, Bobby?

—Aye.

Raj lit the stringy, leafy end to the bidi. He seemed to have difficulty with it; sucking furiously, burning the edge of his thumb, and dampening the butt through more sucking furiously. After much morning struggle, he finally exhaled a few puffs before the green embers died back down to black, and he conceded to stubbing it out in the ashtray. Bobby's gaze was fixed upon him throughout. His friend seemed solemn, perhaps a little disappointed that a cigarette could not burn forever. Raj, feeling hazy and a touch fragile, felt he should lighten the mood by gently breaching Bobby's silence.

—Bit shite those bines, eh?

—Phit?

—Aye, can't even light them.

—Pish.

—Aye, they are pish.

—Nit. Well good, like. Chivey as fuck. Love a chiver.

Bobby sat back against the drapes flowing down bamboo walls in victorious melancholy whilst the others began to chat through the plan for the day. Raj felt Viddy a little distant with him and wondered if he'd overstepped her guard in some way – but it was her guard he loved and so he let it go, as he always did. Liam, lively and buzzed up by morning chai, was vividly espousing the merits of riding back west for the day to the Golden Temple in Amritsar, gesticulating a possible route with his biro and crumpled pocket roadmap. The remaining days left to reach the Parvati Valley entailed long easterly rides, so, as Liam saw it, they may as well take one last swoop west to Amritsar for a night, before turning back for McLeod Ganj and heading further up and through the winding green holy valleys. Viddy, most experienced on a bike – albeit a 125 run-around – was up for it but shrewd to the possibility of fatigue, bringing it up with Liam between delicate sips of her chai. The rattle of an

Enfield was a charm but could be hard on the body, hands, and mind.

—I mean, yeh, it's a cool plan. But do we want to risk more miles? This place is

so peaceful as well. Could be cool to rest up.

—Vid, Vid, Vid, ma sister, the Golden Temple waits for us.

—Yeh, it could be worth it. It's just...

—A lot? I know. But mibbe we just need to force oorsels oot...

Raj, with the brash but unfounded confidence of a road-trip revolutionary, interrupted.

—Ah, fuck it! When else we gonna go? Let's do it.

A general consensus grew stronger in favour of finishing up their chai, storing any luggage with Samir, and packing light for a day's ride and one overnight stay in Amritsar. Liam crumpled the roadmap back inside his pocket, Viddy begin to wind up her hair with one hand, and Raj poured out the last drops of chai, all milky and speckled with herbs. Bobby had not moved or uttered anything during the morning forum, which was not unusual for his self-crafted persona as seer and overseer; but a curious, more sinister tension simmered within him that morning. He kept smoking bidis but finally spoke, not to anyone in particular, but to them all in some stern omniscience.

—I'm nae finished my bine. Also, nae sure if I can be fucked riding another four hours. Fucksake, min.

Bobby gazed downwards towards the bottom ridge of his horn-rimmed spectacles. He sensed unease and winced at his own irritability.

It was precisely because Bobby was so often the lightness that his comments cut through the room. More typically, it was his place to step in with a joke or comment to ease tension, not create it himself, and so a slight paralysis fell upon them all. This was an atypical scene. Liam took it upon himself to burrow through the solemnity.

—Y'sure, Bobby? It's meant to be cool as fuck there.

—Oh, really? Did yiz even ask me? Or just enjoy spikkin around me? Fucksakit.

—Shanti, Bobby, it's all good. Askin yi now then. You good, brother?

—Ach, I'm tired. Sare bones. Sare legs. Sare heid. Nae feeling right. Nae needing to ride a bike. Nae needing to listen to yiz spik around me. But dinna let me stop yiz!

—Naw, man! Leave no man or woman behind, brother! We'll chill. Shanti.

—Nah, nah, at's pish. Me spoiling the day.

—Course not, ma man. We'll chill.

—Ach. Listen, is there a train? Bus? I'm just nae feeling masel and want to avoid the bike, ken. But I'll sit and gaze oot the window a whiley, like...

After a trudging walk back up the gravel path to speak to Samir about travel options, they decided to take the bus to Pathankot, then board a direct train for Amritsar.

A night away from the Bullets could be nice, as could the railroad.

Bobby felt his chest tighten.

The jolting motions of the Pathankot–Amritsar train could be described as serpent-like if it were not for the mechanical and unmuscular regularity of clatter, clang, and movement.

As the train snaked south in syncopated rhythms, its carriages alternately glided left and right, causing the bodies within to sway in unconscious union. On the advice of Samir, Liam had bartered for first-class AC tickets ("most comfort comfort, my friend") but wondered if he was being swindled into doing a turn for Samir's friend, who sold the tickets. It was a sceptical mistrust ingrained in Liam; equal parts helpful in unfamiliar terrain, but also occasionally hindering the possibility of a more authentic form of trust and friendship. Nonetheless, it worked out well, which was, he thought, a lesson in itself.

The carriage was sparsely peppered with polished clientele, evident from flashing glimpses of gold-leaf satin-saris, rubics, sparkling bangles, and well-groomed children with oily black hair partings. There was also a scattering of travelling businessmen; suits, silk turbans, and strikingly white-cotton kaftans. The carriage was convertible as a sleeper, which meant that, when not folded down to create beds, the seating arrangement comprised six persons per compartment, with three blue leather seats facing one another and a fold-down steel table in between for chai and snacks.

Bobby was crammed into the window seat, limbs overlapping with Viddy beside him, whose limbs overlapped with Raj on the aisle seat. Liam took the opposite aisle seat and found himself in quick conversation with the passengers next to him; Fazridun, a stout man in immaculate cotton kaftan and bejewelled cap, and Jagvir, a distinguished-looking Sikh man with curling white whiskers at the summit of a flowing beard. Fazridun, a charismatic hotelier from Amritsar, was particularly chatty with his new-found travelling companions, describing the everyday running of the numerous hotels and guesthouses he owned. They might even stay in one upon arrival; he assured them a favourable arrangement, for it was nice to make new friends. Fazridun's posture was brusque and burly, but comic undertones underlay every sentence spoken in the baritone soundbites directed towards Liam.

—I do two things in life, my friend. Meet and eat. Eat with the people I meet. Meet with people to eat. Such is the hotel business. And you? What is life for you?

—We're just travellin aboot. Students from Scotland. Well, aye, I mean we're based in Scotland usually.

—Ah Scotland! Good whisky in my hotels. Black Label, Balvenie... but not for me. Business only. But here, let us eat and meet!

Fazrudin placed a large brown paper bag on the table, grease stains soaking the bottom and the tips of aloo tikki protruding from the top. The smell was oily and spicy and sensational. With a wry smile, Jagvir entered the conversation, introducing himself by pulling a slim half bottle of Black Label from under his seat. With dignified poise, he gently made an offering to Viddy.

—Scotland, uh? Who better to share with me? Passes the time, no? Shall we?

—Course, we'd love some! Cups or bottle?

—Ah, sweet dear, we are all friends here, no? Welcome to Punjab. Not India, no. Punjab. Scottish, Muslim, Sikh, Hindu, same. Punjab welcomes you here.

Viddy pulled the bottle across the table whilst Raj began to tell Jagvir that his dad was Punjabi too; but the Sikh man seemed nonplussed and more focussed on the bottle and a prospective game of dice. Bobby hadn't flinched throughout, gazing stoically out of the window, tapping his right knuckles against it in some knowing rhythm. Raj felt a slight unease towards Viddy's fast-drinking way of making new friends. They hadn't been drinking much on the trip, mindful of early morning rides and afternoon crashes. As such, it was unnerving, for Raj at least, to see their calm guards drop loose into decadence. Viddy's unexpected breaks from austerity fanned flames of both love and fear in Raj. It reminded him of one of the first nights out in Glasgow they had together. He'd met Viddy a few times, usually in the quiet serenity of a pub where she would quietly join him after orchestra practice, violin rucksack double-strapped across her shoulders. An understated elegance pervaded her gentle gait; she came across as quiet, thoughtful, and as if her favourite pastime was collecting rare books and scouring special collections. All those things were true, but it came as far more of a shock to Raj when he saw her spinning on her head to NWA later that night; pupils dilating, pulse racing, and headed to a high-rise afterparty in Clydebank after the club shut. He was never sure if it was rebellion against caste, family, or a rebuttal of gendered constraints. Or maybe just a surprising facet to a complex, beautiful being who maintained mystique without ever alienating others. It was her ambiguity and multi-dimensionality that he was drawn to. Or perhaps he was drawn to her comfort with ambiguity. Something he had always lacked.

Gentle joviality evolved into raucous laughter as the mechanical serpent swung the travelling companions and their dice back and forth across the fold-down table. Viddy and Fazridun were particularly animated, holding cubicle court, whilst Jagvir wore a wide but dignified smile through-out, apparently amused by the untypical circumstances of, for him, a typically tiresome train ride to Amritsar. Raj kept a watchful eye on Bobby, who'd said he wasn't feeling up to drinking nor the game, despite Fazrudin's polite insistence that dice was best played sober anyway. Instead, Bobby sipped chai and coiled his body into the window, head lean-ing against the glass pane, catching occasional beams of sunlight, blurry fields, cows; some signs of peace and quiet to swallow the feeling of everything weighing too heavily, too tight in his chest. The dice game came to an end – Faz-rudin was victorious, and the others shuffled around and recalibrated themselves and their snacks for the remainder of the journey. Viddy brushed past Raj as Jagvir squeezed his knees in to make room. She shuffled down the aisle, but her angry exclamation soon jolted the others into anger and panic. A flash of chaos in the confines of a carriage.

—Get your hands off me, you little prick!

A silk-shirted young businessman with oily, cheek-length hair had pawed at Viddy's torso, asking her if she'd like another drink with him in the toilet. She needed no saving from a male seediness well known to her, but fren-zied reinforcements arrived without request or want. Liam came first, barrelling down the train like a bulldog, nostrils flaring, ready to play the madman, accent accentuated, growling and prowling towards his prey.

—Fuck ya daein, ya wee fuckin dick! Al fuckin glass fuck oot yer wee slimy fuckin face, ya wee fuckin...

Viddy stepped back into the aisle shocked, affronted, and slightly concerned as Liam, small but ferocious when pro-voked, gripped his hands around the slimy businessman's neck. The man's eyes widened in fear, arms convulsing in a plea, before Liam loosened his grip as Fazrudin and Jagivr arrived on the scene, each wearing big-browed frowns. With almost symmetrical, wild gesticulations of heads and hands, they sternly scolded the man in Punjabi, apparently demanding he get off the train. Amidst their anger, they wore a forlorn look in between shouts, seemingly feeling embarrassed or responsible in some way for the man's actions. Viddy felt even more affronted, more annoyed, and raked a hand down the front of her face. Then, before the man could scurry into the next carriage, Raj appeared and his reaction sparked a tense exchange with Viddy.

—Excuse me! Did you touch my girlfriend? What did you do?

—Raj, God, I'm not your fucking girlfriend!

—What did he do, Vid? Fucking little shit. Tell me. What did he do?

—For fuck's sake, Raj! Can everyone just shut the fuck up!

Viddy cut through the chaos, and the man scurried off. Adrenaline and aggression and hearts pulped with the clangs of the mechanical serpent. Bobby was nowhere to be seen during the furore, having bolted down the carriage in the opposite direction. It had all gotten too much. An inner monologue of possibly verbalised thoughts spun through him as he shakily ambled down the carriage, chest tightening, legs weaker. It was too much responsibility to bear. Bad things could happen. Maybe he didn't tap the window enough times. Pangs of fear from the past compounded the present. He saw himself from above the mechanically snaking train and his chest got tighter. The air was harder to breathe. Everyone was staring at him. Or maybe they weren't. It was impossible to tell. He needed off.

Bobby hyperventilated through one carriage to the next as the train slowed momentarily when it passed through a station. It didn't stop but screeched to a mechanical rhythm slow enough for him to throw one leg out of the open carriage door onto the platform, causing his body to uncoil away from the train. He landed back-first on the dusty concrete, legs splayed, breaths heavy, but relief coursing through him. From his earthy vantage point, he glanced up at the slowly receding train carriages. Iron bars, open windows, and large rusted wheels were pulling into the distance. Along a rectangular middle strip of open-air barred windows, he made out three figures ambling and scrambling in the opposite direction to the train, limbs flailing and little heads occasionally flicking in his direction. They made it to the rear open door of the fast-receding carriage, poured out onto the platform in a bundle of limbs and flying satchels and panic, then collapsed a few yards ahead of Bobby. It was Raj, Viddy, and Liam.

The four of them slumped up against a cool stone platform wall and listened to the train rumble into the distance. The humid, sun-filled air was stagnating, and tension rose among them. Bodies lacked will, bonds felt fractured, and dullness displaced the bright blue sky with gathering clouds; a thunderstorm beckoned. Viddy clasped both hands across the crown of her head, tilting it skywards.

—What a shitshow. Also, what was all that aggro about? Knights in fucking shining armour, over here. You think I'm not used to shit like that?

Raj put one hand over her curled-up knee.

—We were just worried. Well, I was anyway.

—Why? You think I can't handle that? It's nothing! Nothing.

—That's not true, Viddy. You shouldn't put up with...

—Don't fucking tell me what I should and shouldn't. You have no idea. No idea.

—I'm sorry, Viddy. Just after that shit you put up with at Joginder Nagar...

—Oh, I "put up" with it, did I? Just stop. Stop. Stop. Stop. Shut up. We should all still be on that train. Whole lot of drama for nothing. Chimp behaviour. An insult to chimp behaviour. And where the fuck are we now, anyway?

They looked across the train tracks. There was a line of desolate square concrete buildings lined with people sleeping under the shade of them. The honks and shouts and revs of traffic sounded to their rear, and a sign at the end of the platform was comprised of nailed bits of wood pointing place names in unclear directions.

FUN IN SUN PALACE

GURDAWAR

TRAFFIC PARK

PIZZA BITE

SADAR BAZAR

Liam blew out his cheeks, before deflating in face and spirit.

—Fuck knows, man. Here, Bobby, where were yi during that shitstorm? How'd yi end up oot the train, anyway?

—Wisnae feelin masel.

—Y'awrite?

—Hale hing wiz ma fault.

—Whit?

—Bad shit follows me aroond.

—Naw, Bobby. It wiz just a wee slimy arsehole. Whityae on?

—Da ken. Shit just closes in sometimes. Cah help it.

—Here, mate, take a drink of water. Yer probably tired, eh? Heat. Exhaustion. It's tough, man.

—Aye. mibbe. Wisnae nice.

—Yer cool, man. Take a few breaths, eh.

The unfurling revelation of Bobby's turmoil eased the tension among them a little. It was jarring, even sad, to see their source of amusement succumb to exhaustion, sipping back water as beads of sweat cascaded from his pores causing an occasional shiver. It was getting cooler, the clouds swirled darker, and rain threatened. Viddy pushed herself upwards, using Raj's shoulder as springboard and crutch. The contact felt nice to him. Peaceable, like the warm glance she gave Bobby as he began to open up to her.

—Ken this is ma first time oota Scotland? Travelled loads in ma mind, right enough. But this is the first in body. Been amazin, like. But am ready fir hame.

—Well, guess your first trip might be a memorable one? I'm not sure I feel ready to go – in a way it's as if we only just arrived now. This feeling of being present. It's like it's taken the whole trip to actually find it. And now that we're here, we have to go.

—Nae want to go back like?

—Happy to go back, sad to leave. It's different for me,

y'know? Going back. It's not going home. Hame. Whatever you want to call it. But I actually feel way more at peace with that now. Like, I can be anywhere, and I want to go everywhere. It's liberating. For so long, I was so uncomfortable with rootless uncertainty. The impossibility of all possibilities is so fucking scary sometimes. Where to be, live, belong to. I see it more as a blessing now.

Raj smiled quietly to himself, looking down at crushed bidi butts on the platform. He felt Viddy's special kind of truth. It was inspiring, and he knew from that moment that he would let go, let her be; realising that longing and love and lust probably wasn't love at all. His special kind of truth was different. He was less sure that he wasn't going home. But that was fine. In that moment. It was fine. And fuck it. There was a whole lot more to come. He turned to Viddy.

—Aye, hear yi, Vids. I came here thinking I'd find a way to connect to the place. But, actually, I don't need a place at all. I feel the strongest I've ever felt about that. Am ready for wherever opens its arms. Where I come from, or where I'm supposed to imagine I come from. It means nothing anymore. And there's so much to see.

Liam shot up, walking over to the platform edge, looking up the tracks in a mixture of wonder and dishevelment.

—Fuck me, man. The schemes to this.

Raj smiled.

—Does it seem far away? That past?

—Naw, man. It's in me, man. Always will be. Young team don't die, yo. It's changed, but. Ah don't hate the past anymore. It's freeing. Like Vid says. It's like an invincibility. And fuck it. Why not, eh?

—Aye. We've got it all ahead of us.

—That we do, man. The road is long.

By this time, Bobby had calmed himself and sparked a bidi. He looked up to Liam after a long and profound exhalation of mystical clouds.

—Aye. It's nae at fuckin long when we da ken where we are. How we gettin hame?

Liam pirouetted around, hands in the air, shouting.

—Where's hame! Where the fuck is hame, anyways, ma man!

Bobby looked up, smiling.

—Aiberdeen, min! Scotland.

—Aye, it's gonnae be exciting tae be back. Better days ahead, man.

—Aye. We can be those better days. Am ready, like.

—Aye? Moan the Boaby! Dream as if yi live in the early days of FUN IN SUN FUCKIN PALACE...

They laughed and shook and laughed some more, bodies on the platform, clouds gathering above. Viddy sat back down beside Bobby, leaning against his shoulder, speaking gently.

—Look, shall we just get a taxi back to McLeod Ganj? Chill out for a few days. There's no rush to get to Parvati Valley. Or anywhere, really.

—Taxi? Be a fortune, eh?

—Nah, we'll split it. It won't be bad.

—Nae Golden Temple?

—Ach. Bad omens for me now. Let's chill. Head back to Samir's.

—Diz sound good, like.

—Let's do it.

The four of them traipsed to the end of the platform and exited through a revolving steel door, which spun into the wailing noise of the station car park. Following a relatively quick haggle with a Brylcreemed, cowboy-shirted, young taxi driver, they headed back north. Liam sat in the front, chatting whisky and Elvis Presley with the driver; whilst Viddy, Raj, and Bobby began to sway in and out of a deep sleep in the back. Rain chattered heavier on the windows, wipers squeaked louder, and "If I Can Dream" fuzzed out the cassette player. The ceremonial trumpet piped them back to peace. The light burned brighter in the darkened sky. Birds were flying higher. Gales of promise howled amidst the rain.

They would be back in McLeod Ganj in under an hour, a greater truth between them born in adversity.

A gentle breeze floated through the valley, unfurling hot ribbons of light from crackling timber blocks fast transforming to transient dust. Rest fell upon them naturally, or perhaps by necessity. They would head for Delhi in the morning, and fly back in three days; not necessarily for home, but for life back in Glasgow, for a while at least.

Raj and Liam had awkwardly pulled mattresses from the sparsely furnished Parvati River cottage outside, arranging them around the firepit which stood between them and a flowing estuary. The cottage had a balcony that extended over the river, supported by large wooden stilts that plunged into the gently flowing water, then disappeared. After the chaos of Delhi, the failed trip to Amritsar, a limb-rumbling ride from McLeod Ganj, and a final dance with the Shaivites, it had been the perfect place to be still for a few days.

The ashtray was ashy, and the even ashier remains of incense faded in streaks and dots and particles across the timber balcony flooring. On their last night in the valley, though, it seemed better to be outside. Beside the fire. Leaping flames. Lapping water. They topped the mattresses with paisley-patterned blankets from the cottage's singular bamboo cupboard. The blankets overlapped and curled into one another, smoothing the angular arrangement of adjacent mattress-ends to form a circle, warm and glowing in the early evening dusklight. Circular lanterns, attached by frayed strings to the balcony roof, began to gently sway in the breeze, and the luminosity of red tubular lights, which lined the architectural outline of the cottage walls, began to emerge as the sky fell lower. The cottage was glowing. They were glowing. And in the crackling glow of this imperfect, paisley-patterned circle, the four of them spoke together in the rare occurrence of collective hope and optimism towards past, future, present. It didn't matter whether it was fate or just chaos that had determined, or would determine, what came before and after. Thoughts, decisions, words – none of them were futile, not even in the face of a world already written.

The world inside of themselves.

The everything, and the nothing.

LIEUTENANT LIAM

Who are they?
These people we meet.
These people we laugh with,
love, kiss, remember, grieve, kill, forget;
or just pass on the street, sit next to on the bus,
or ride pillion with for a summer. These people. In the
mind, these people take on some undefinable significance that
is infinite and eternal yet also, sometimes, fleeting. These people.
Sometimes these people come charged as symbols, and other times they
appear disconnected and peripheral but remain no less symbolic. These
people come back to nothing special. These people combine to form
occult and prophetic constellations of ourselves. Futures and
pasts that might one day be written so that our fleeting
mortality might cast some small shadowy imprint of
forgotten pasts. Particles. Fragments. People.
These people only become real when
they become ghosts. The
Kirtankara reunite on
the Isle of Skye.

○

They met outside the Co-op in Kyle of Lochalsh. Raj and Bobby caught the train from Glasgow, Viddy hopped on the bus down from Staffin, and James gave Liam a lift up in the white HGV he'd kitted out for lugging bikes around the country; JF Auto Services logo emblazoned in green capital letters on the sides. A colourful ode to the Hoops.

Bobby looked stoic, balanced by the ivory horn across his chest and the old harmonium box roped to his back. It had been a while since he felt protected by his spiritual tortoise shell. He was glad he remembered to grab it before they left his flat. Raj leant against the stained pebbledash wall, smoking. Viddy was calm, restrained, and had neatly pleated her hair, which flowed down each shoulder. The lorry creaked to a halt, and the engine belched a fizzy burp. Liam skipped down the steps wearing black cons and a tight leather jacket. His wee nostrils were flaring, smile wide and toothy.

—S'happenin, fuckers! Right, James gonnae help me and Viddy unload the bikes. Raj, sort oot the smokes n whisky, eh? Bobby, mate, you high? You've no moved an inch, n what the fuck is that oann yer chest? Class, mate. Looks class, anyway. Fuckin yas. Here wi fuckin go, ehh!

James and Viddy rolled the Royal Enfield Bullets down the extended ramps. Liam's oppressive excitement was a welcome distraction from small talk and the anxiety of reunion. There was a collective unease amongst them.

Nobody had greeted one another, aside Raj and Bobby, who chatted a bit on the train ride up in between shite Scotrail coffee and Walkers crisps. Liam's assault of excited conversation masked the nervousness inside of himself. He'd exchanged a few texts with Raj in the past week about meeting up, but the abrupt replies had sent him spinning.

Raj! Brother! Ready for the trip?

Hi Liam. Yeh. Be nice to see everyone again.

Cool man! What time yi think yous will be at Kyle of Lochalsh?

Not sure yet mate. Keep you posted.

Liam couldn't ever remember Raj calling him "mate" before. It was disconcerting. Strange how a term of overt friendship could stir up paranoia like that. Liam also couldn't tell if Raj was unenthused or maybe just busy with work. He was probably reading way too much between the lines of these mundane messages anyway. Fuck it, he thought. Maybe it was because he still didn't have a job, partner, or kids, and was the only one with enough time on his hands to care. Fuck it. May as well just get on and enjoy it. Not overthink it all. The only way to do that would be to turn up and whip up the positive energy. Get the young team back together. Get the tunes on. Bikes revved. Whisky passed. But why did it all feel so fragile? Fuck it. May as well just get on and enjoy it and not overthink it all.

If Liam's nervous energy manifested an excited chatter, Raj felt himself fall into a stoic sense of anxiety over what to say. He didn't know where to start and was immediately paralysed by his own folly for ever thinking this was a worthwhile idea. The drifting, the distance from his old friends, seemed too hard recover. Raj's chest felt tighter and tighter as he chain-smoked against the pebbledash Co-op wall, even though he'd given up smoking months ago. Bobby was the most composed in the car park, observing his thoughts but not reacting or letting his body boom into anxiety. He assumed the trip was mainly about Viddy. Something to take her mind off John's death. And besides, he wanted to ride pillion. He'd be Nicholson, she'd be Fonda. He'd remembered his helmet, and there was whisky in his ivory horn. Be way more fun than before. Less pressure.

Viddy, peering out the bus window from Staffin, had thought the ride would be good for Bobby. She'd felt pangs of guilt over the last few years. She never visited him in hospital, or even talked to him about his diagnosis. She was caught up with John, the twins, crofting, and there was inherent discomfort in facing up to the ghosts of a past she'd left behind. She and Liam had also been texting each other about Raj needing a break for a few days. Raj's wife, Ibti, was seven months pregnant; but they knew from Raj's silence on the matter that he was probably overwhelmed, uncertain, haunted by the trappings of a life he was certain to live but wholly uncertain about. Viddy assumed that the very thought of family life in London suburbia would trouble Raj. He'd carved his identity as a free spirit, a traveller, someone who always wanted to be seen taking the road less travelled, sticking it to the man and mortgages and babies and security. Yet here he was now: Communications Officer at HM Department for Digital, Culture, Media and Sport, recent homeowner, and painting a spare room with moon and star stencils in time for the new arrival.

Raj and Viddy had probably drifted furthest apart, which may well have been a consequence of their past awkwardness, and the tendency we all have to kill the people we once felt for intensely. They could once make you but would now break you. Moving on, leaving things behind. The latter was a lot easier for Viddy, not just because of gods and goddesses and faith and rebirth, but because she never loved Raj like Raj loved her. Or, at least, he thought he did in certain moments of whisky and longing and looking to find a fellow lost soul in search of themselves; only to find out she was never that lost at all but simply more at peace with herself than he could ever be. They had barely spoken since arriving at the Co-op. The cold drizzle presided over the most unceremonious of car park reunions.

The Royal Enfields were lined up, facing towards the exit as James closed up the back of the HGV. Viddy felt relief at the little time left for pleasantries, and Bobby was first to straddle one of the bikes, each with a recently restored chrome petrol tank ribboned with shiny red Royal Enfield lettering. A font, a logo, a logos, from and for another time. Bobby positioned himself, pillion, squatting on the back seat, and slid his old harmonium box around his back to leave enough room up front. Viddy twisted her thick hair around into a tight ball and tucked it under the back of her open-faced helmet, which she pulled on to hear Liam crackling excitedly through the Bluetooth intercom system.

—Here wi fuckin go, *mon ameees*. Ready, eh?

The two of them gently warmed the throttle, droning a gentle bassline as Raj slid on his newly purchased motorcycle gloves and helmet and steadied his own steed, kicking out a gentle rumble on the second go. They didn't wear helmets in India. Back then, he and Viddy used to pleat each other's hair to keep it from blowing across their faces, usually swapping between chillum and weaves while Liam faced off Bobby in a chess match soundtracked by Hari Om Sharan, *Dark Side of The Moon*, and Cohen – always in that order. Raj didn't have much hair left to pleat these days, with his shaved sides and long, wispy dark fringe; responsible enough for Whitehall creative, outlandish enough to suggest previous skins, perhaps. But Hari Om Sharan remained. He was here now, and so were they. The intercom volume bleeped up into a crescendo as Liam primed the others while controlling it from his phone.

—Hari Om, ma man! Hari Om! Ready? Shanti shanti!

The unravelling strings of "Kirtan (Sampati)" rose up and around their helmets, resonating in the car park, changing the movement and light around them. Woodwind notes lifted above the rumble of the stationary bikes, soundtracking an altercation between James and a teenager in a bright green Corsa with a red spoiler attached to the back. The teenager fearfully fleeted, and the HGV pulled right onto the A87. Liam rolled his feet forward, easing his Enfield left towards the bridge; Raj followed, then Viddy with Bobby riding pillion, all Nicholson, all cool. Somewhere between lament, praise, devotion, pain, loss, and ecstasy Sharan's voice rose above the tabla, driving their song onwards. Bells chimed as they pulled out of the car park and past a fleet of Co-op delivery vans. Liam, now free and open and high on the A87, clunked into third gear, and shouted into the intercom. It was a recital. He'd clearly rehearsed.

—*Cleansing the mirror in the form of my mind with the pollen of the lotus-feet of the Guru, I describe the unblemished glory of Rama, which restores the four fruits!* Mon, ya bas!

Distorted crackles over the intercom snuffled a harmonious, raucous, collective laughter they had not heard in years.

Beats, graced by ringing bells, rolling forward, unfurling in song.

O

The Enfields rumbled up the A855 from Portree, headed for The Storr. The single-track road cut through green banks, and cool grey patches flashed across their visors like scenes from a Super 8 film. They flickered on together in a celluloid strip – Liam up top and Bobby bringing up the rear, head raised high like a centurion among the clouds. "The Hanuman Chalisa" echoed faintly in-helmet behind the louder rumbles of three engines pulling along twisty roads.

Bobby, jerking back and forth, let his head fall further back as he caught glimmers of the road behind him, receding into a sharp point of nothingness. He thought about Tulsidas, the poet-saint, penning forty verses to find nothingness in everything. Sometimes, when Bobby walked around cities, he liked to imagine them as empty, desolate spaces in which only churches, cathedrals, temples, synagogues, gurdawaras, and other spaces of devotion remained. Road signs, traffic lights, and rat racers vanished. Black tarmac gave way to grey dust that swirled around in the wind, obscuring his vision, leaving only the ornate spires of holiness above. He would imagine walking into cold, stone cathedrals, letting the silence nurture his sense of absolution from self and world, before surrendering to the call of other people and a spiced pumpkin latte from Costa.

But there was little need to imagine this on Skye, which was already holiness to him in its rugged purity of rock, mist, and green undulations. He didn't want to think too much about how the popular image of the Highlands and Islands clashed with the stark reality of life there. It's true, the yogi-herbalists, second-home wankers, and diarists who visited briefly then wrote extensively, often knew nothing of life there – but why couldn't *he* have his own moment of romance? This was a holy moment in a holy place. Holy holy holy. He was older now – it *could* be holy. He remembered reading *Waverley* as an undergraduate, and feeling enchanted by Flora's singing, her harping a Highland air by a waterfall, mist on the mountain, dark on the vale. He also remembered being laughed at by a university lecturer in Tennent's Bar for lapping it up. Apparently, it was a twee and fabricated construction of landscape, people, and nation. Ridiculous to buy into it, apparently. Bobby, silently sensitive, felt hurt, fragile, and inept. But it didn't stop his occasional solo wanderings in the Highland and Islands; sitting by misty brooks wondering if his Doric strains might be welcome over Bardic pluckings. He was soon conditioned not to reveal that he was conditioned by romance, for wouldn't that be embarrassing? Bobby breathed deeply, one hand on his horn to keep it from swaying, the other on the back handle of the motorcycle. He closed his eyes. Less intellect, more romance. That was okay.

A dark peak in the distance radiated purple. Viddy clunked down into second as the road wound round an earthy bank to reveal a narrow stretch of silvery water. "Shree Durga Chalisa" pulsed through their helmets, chorus sounding like it was sung by a million or more voices before.

Viddy had always enjoyed the view of life and landscape through the lens of motorcycle rides. Moving images offset by flickers, fragmentations, and fuzz. Some moments, features, people, or objects would appear prominently – a scarved elderly woman posting a letter, an open gate, a red roadside telephone box – while others seem to contract and blur into an unknowable mesh of motion that was there, gone, and past in a peripheral flicker of memory. She had forgotten this perception. Everything was so linear these days. The twins rooted her in the moment. The rabid macaroni fights, lullabies, moments of mourning, tears, sleep, and waking to see if the hens had eggs. The problem with her rootedness, her linearity, her mindful presence of daily action and being, was John. There was no space or place for him in the linear order of living. The more she tried to conjure a clear picture of his face, his gait, his voice, his smell, the more her memory failed her. The more she wanted it to fail her. He was fading further and further away, leaving her with nothing but the present, and she was numb to memory, numb to the past.

Viddy pulled the throttle and leant her right knee into the corner, straightening herself before shaking into a jolt of fear as she saw a head appear at the right side of her helmet. At first, she thought she was daydreaming and swiftly gripped the handlebars in concentration – for if India taught them many things, one was to stay focused on the bike. Just ask Bobby about the goat. But she soon realised that her will to focus was obscuring a heightened awareness of herself and her body, as they began distorting, refracting, and evolving in fluid motion on the silvery surface of Loch Fada, which had transformed into a cinematic funhouse mirror at the side of the road. She caught a breath, eased the throttle and dropped back into second, tilting her head right to see the slender body of water which contained her.

Body of Water
Moving
John's Body
Full of Water
Water of Body
Bodies of Water
Fluid
Refracting
Moving
Evolving
Motion

Viddy caught herself whispering but she couldn't remember what, and she hoped the intercom didn't pick up anything. She and John used to stop at this spot on still clear nights to watch the reflection of stars glisten on the loch, but she had avoided it since. There was little point in dredging up memories and sifting through love that had turned to pain. Little point in feeling fragile for the sake of it. Little point in remembering. As usual, she didn't stop, but kept the bike rolling slow. She began tracing the blurry outline of the two bodies beside her. They sometimes appeared transparent. Green hillsides rolled across the two bodies, only she wasn't sure what was illusion and what was real, as the flow of images combined into one moment in which she could not be sure of anything. The bodies were superimposed on the loch, and the hills on the bodies, and all these unrelated images appeared transparent but bold, clear but intangible, and melted into something she found inexplicably beautiful, for a very brief moment at least. The intoxication of the mirror, the body of water, began to gently sober as the landscape dimmed further into dark greys, the occasional orange blot adding flourishes of colour to the falling dusklight.

They had left the Co-op later than expected, raced through Portree, but had now caught sight of the old man, The Storr. Up ahead, Raj's bike was trundling closely behind Liam, who, by his erratic, unpredictable standards, had led a fairly gentle, meandering peloton up the east coast of the island. Unlike the others, Liam loved the buzz of ripping back the throttle, but also caught himself cruising slowly at times, eyes down, letting his vision relax into seeing motions of sharp and then blurred and then sharp and then blurred rolls of the rubber tire. He was drawn to the circularity, the rhythm, sound, and strange awareness of physically moving somewhere while sitting still. He recalled a famous picture of Gandhi, all ribs, collarbones, contemplation, reading by his charkha and home-spun linen. He wondered why pictures like that leave such large imprints on our memory, perhaps a visual form of eulogy that encapsulates the essence of someone or something they experienced. The imprisoned martyr making his own clothes; the intellectual man in meditative practice. Perhaps we all leave visual eulogies. But he wondered what his might look like, and he felt sad. The light dimmed further, and melancholy strings from Sharan's "Japle Hari Ka Naam Sannjh Sakare" bellowed around Liam's helmet as his thoughts spun in tandem with the wheels below. It seemed to him like these hills had heard faint echoes of these strings before; laments for love, for land, for kin. Similar sounds in different mounds. It felt wholesome and, for the first time since setting off, Liam, ever concentrated on leading the charge, eased the throttle, and eased his thoughts into a more lucid space as dusk grew darker.

A few months ago, Liam had received one of those chain emails from a distant cousin in Australia, with a bold subject line in capital letters that read A REASON, A SEASON, A LIFETIME. He was simultaneously shaken, frustrated, and embarrassed by the fact he'd been so affected by such a terrible fucking poem. Raj would surely rip him if he knew, but still, with wheels rolling up towards The Storr, he found himself reciting those first few lines:

People come into your life for a reason,
*   a season or a lifetime.*
When you figure out which one it is,
*   you will know what to do for each person.*

He couldn't remember the rest properly, but he had become unexpectedly troubled by the infinite possibilities of reasons or seasons or lifetimes. What a shit fuckin poem, man. But it bothered him. It bothered him how shit the poem was. And it bothered him how much he was bothered by the shit poem. And it bothered him to think about Raj, and probably Bobby too, laughing if he brought up how bothered he actually was. Especially because he also felt bothered by who his reasons, seasons, and lifetimes actually were. This was the underside to Liam's confidence, authority, and gallus feet forward in life. He worked hard to feel free from attack, from ridicule; a culturally acquired defensive mechanism, which paradoxically plagued what he gave to others. It was draining to maintain, which probably explained the gear back in the day, then later the meditation, the yoga, the silent retreats, and most recently the Vipassanā meditation instructor course. There was an expectation, for all reasons and seasons, of cocky assuredness that left him vulnerable; and that fragility perpetually simmered under the witty quips.

Remnants of the shit poem echoed against the closing bells of Sharan's lament, which lingered throughout his dusky ruminations. Liam felt irked. He'd just read a Martin Hägglund book especially in time for the trip in the hope of conversation, inspiration, and ideas from the others, only to be foiled by obsessively thinking about some spam email. It reminded him of power ballads. All that Proust, de Beauvoir, Barthes, and Cohen. In the toilet. All those theoretical seminar musings over centuries' worth of knowledge thrust into the void of time by five minutes of Foreigner's "I Want to Know What Love Is". Liam remembered hearing it on his Amsterdam layover, all smoky swimming eyes in some dive bar opposite Centraal with two mannequins behind the bar and a neon jukebox. The eerie opening synth and electronic snare drum boomed out as Liam began to question love. What mountain must he climb to know it? The question weighed heavy on his shoulders, but the rousing chorus allowed him to see through the neon clouds.

Love. It keeps him warm, but he doesn't have it. He only sees it. No, he thinks he sees it. And this is what keeps him warm as life grows colder, not the attainment of it. The lover's fatal identity is precisely this, the one who waits for it, the one who always waits, to know what it actually is. But it's the *belief* that he can actually be shown it that sustains the amorous infatuation of embrace. Liam wanted to know what love was. He wanted to be shown. He wanted to feel. He knew he could be shown. He knew he was thinking too hard.

Those lyrics and that music was someplace else. There was little point in consciously trying to retrieve what it meant. Better to listen to the reverberations of the present. The final chimes of "Japle Hari Ka Naam Sannjh Sakare" faded into engine noise, and Liam kicked down gears like an old jukebox in between songs.

—How yizaw haudin up, *mon freres*? Or *moi freres and sere*, eh?

He glanced down to see Raj, a small, blurry dark shape in the centre of his mirror, and an even smaller Viddy, drifting right and left, beyond the mirror rims, head tilted towards the loch, with Bobby's beak perked skywards just behind her.

The mirror glass was dimming, fogging up, pears of hope trickling down.

He thought they were close, but it was hard to see what was behind him.

WHY DON'T YOU TRY?

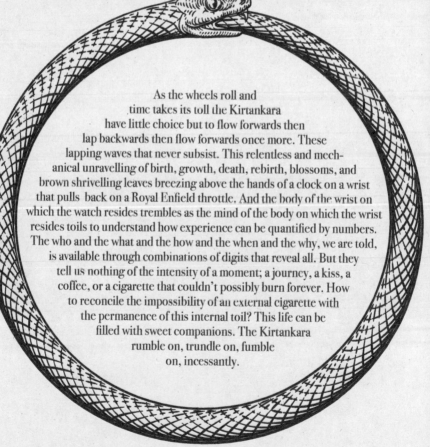

As the wheels roll and
time takes its toll the Kirtankara
have little choice but to flow forwards then
lap backwards then flow forwards once more. These
lapping waves that never subsist. This relentless and mechanical unravelling of birth, growth, death, rebirth, blossoms, and
brown shrivelling leaves breezing above the hands of a clock on a wrist
that pulls back on a Royal Enfield throttle. And the body of the wrist on
which the watch resides trembles as the mind of the body on which the wrist
resides toils to understand how experience can be quantified by numbers.
The who and the what and the how and the when and the why, we are told,
is available through combinations of digits that reveal all. But they
tell us nothing of the intensity of a moment; a journey, a kiss, a
coffee, or a cigarette that couldn't possibly burn forever. How
to reconcile the impossibility of an external cigarette with
the permanence of this internal toil? This life can be
filled with sweet companions. The Kirtankara
rumble on, trundle on, fumble
on, incessantly.

O

With the coming of a darker light, Liam kept returning to the dream of what he was or what he thought he was. Trundling along, Bullet piercing through dusk, the possibilities of the past and future haunted him. He wondered if it haunted the others as much as himself. Strong personalities, wide ones, require strong strains of memory. There had to be some way of weaving a narrative of self; some way to connect the past to this very moment. It's the only way he could ever be real. For what else did he have to give? He caught a glimpse of what he'd been looking for, at that moment at least, in his mirror glass.

—Right, *mon ameees*, Jamesy's caught up wi us. We're almost there.

The folly, deep folly, of letting Liam loose on an intercom system that allowed for him to speak without reply pulsed through the others. Bobby and Viddy grumbled uncomfortable questions to one another, craning their necks left and right to hear each other over the Bullet's meditative rumble. Ahead of them, Raj felt an uneasy pang that sank down from his helmet and into his chest. Nobody knew James was coming on the trip beyond dropping the bikes off. It felt ominous. It sounded like Liam had somewhere to be. But it was hard to tell where any of them should be.

A miniature white HGV careered across the top left-hand corner of Viddy's rear-view mirror, looming larger and closer and more imposing by the minute. She could just about make out James's tanned dome in the middle of a dark strip above the large grill plate, but perhaps that was imagined too. The little details so often are. Viddy had caught up to Raj, who was now closely tailing Liam, the three bikes snaking around slowly, as if in some cautious dance. Liam hadn't said anymore but pulled down on his Bullet, gradually bending it right up a track towards a cottage in the dusky distance with two columns and a grand portico. Tailing the convoy, James's HGV fizzed, belched, and bumped its way over the potholes, taking up the entirety of the track. The Royal Enfield engines trickled out staccato murmurs. The night darkened further. The portico glowed. And the tension rose. Raj pulled off his helmet, ruffling up a hen mess of sweaty thin hair, before turning wearily to Liam.

—What's going on, man? James? This place? Thafuck.

Bobby and Viddy let Raj figure out the situation, perching themselves on a stonewall dyke adjacent to the bikes and James's imposing HGV, which was parked haphazardly in front of the strange croft building, glowing like some neoclassical ode to feudalism. Someone opened the oak-tiled door. Raj grew nervous. Viddy seemed entertained. She and John had never taken this track.

It was nice to be on new ground.

Raj and Liam were close around the time they went to India, almost infatuated with one another. The strange and beautiful bliss of heterosexual desire and friendship, when men love each other in a manner uncomplicated by sex and lust.

Bobby, never jealous and deeply perceptive, assumed their attraction was one of wants and absences. He thought they each desired some aspect of each other's soul, being, body. Perhaps all friendships, relationships, and interactions of a positively glowing kind are like that.

Raj was immediately alluring to Liam the moment his aloof skinny frame, flares, and pleated hair fell in beside him at Gilmorehill lecture theatre. Liam's decision to do an access course was a wild scratch at another possible self. He wanted away for a while. To learn more about books, reading, and to meet, love, and lust beyond his tight family circle and childhood friends who were more like family anyway. In Raj he met, for a while at least, the embodiment of a free-willed wanderer with nothing to lose and everything to explore. Threaded bracelets, beads, cool music; there was a beatnik trapped inside Liam, and maybe it was Raj. Some blissful simpatico emerged from the moment they decided to go for a smoke in Kelvingrove Park after the lecture.

While Liam was attracted by Raj's Bohemian aloofness, it was, ironically, Liam's very rootedness in Glasgow, or being *fae Glesgae* and all that entails, that seduced Raj. Through his own shortcomings, frustrations, and Freudian lacks, Raj was fascinated by the salience of place in relation to Liam's identity and the people around him – James, Rhona, even wee Ashlene. Pure weegies, min. Pure. Must be nice to be pure and proud, he thought. It not only provided a plinth with which to view the world, but also made past and future selves possible. Whether it was through belonging, aversion, entrapment, escape or otherwise, Liam's idea of himself as a boy *fae Glesgae* was internalised, encoded in his skin. Raj was seduced by this authenticity of belonging, and even misbelonging. Liam took him to the pubs "up north" – gravelly ayes, silent pints, chib marks on cheeks. Hauf pints and nips and chats about his papa, who was meant to have been a real Calton razor king. The 'Tic showed Raj people didn't need to know each other to know common oppression and rebellion; and fuck, man, Liam's uncle had even pulled on the hood a few times, supposedly. Grim stuff. Still worth talking about. Still worth bonding over. It was enthralling. Rooted. Real. A revelation for someone with little sense of self or place or history.

Later on, though, Raj grew sceptical, disenchanted, even disappointed by the salience of place. Everything Liam said became a trope. He was kind to old ladies on the bus. That's just what it was like *in Glesgae*, eh. *Only in Glesgae*, eh. He was becoming more interested in the arts; the city was a *hotbed of culture*, for sure, but mind the men who built this city, eh? *Men wi a trade*. All that was fun, games, jelly, and ice cream until the tropes became threatening – usually when Liam was feeling lost and needed something to hold onto, like the period just after graduation. Peace and joviality gave way to violence, like it so often does at the midnight circus of Sauchiehall Street on a Saturday. One night Bobby had a few boys down from the Shire. Bumpkins, choochters – nice burly loons. A nicht oot in the big smoke, checked shirts and bootcut Levi's, shots, chunders then kebabs after a smoky night in The Garage. But some wee neds got all up in the glasses of Bobby in the kebab shop queue. The "speccy cunt" wiz ripe for rippin. Bobby and the burly loons played it calm, up until the point one of the wee guys dropped a slice of pizza, which Bobby picked up and ate, to their laughter, disgust, and aggravation. A toxic combination of expressive attributes.

—Eatin that aff the flair, ya speccy prick?

—Aye. Ate yer ma aff the flair last night ana!

Bobby got nutted and lost a tooth, which he never replaced, for he felt it would taint the memory. The body should remember these things. But it was Liam's reaction that night that left the others most shaken. Blood, shards, and a lot of remorse the next morning. It was like he had to show the wee guys, and the big burly bootcut bumpkins, who he was. Where he *was fae*, fucksake. What he was capable of, fucksake. It was hard to watch. Hard to be around. Dark. Violent. Unnecessary, but necessary. Instinctual, but curated. A civic red mist long forecast.

Then there was the incident down the Gallowgate a few months later. Initially Liam tried to reassure Raj. Just selling a bit of puff. It's nothin, fucksake. And *nae cunt fucks with the McManamans* anyway. Until somebody did fuck with Liam and Raj, and James showed up with a hammer and left some poor bastard with broken hands for their trouble. It was hard to know if people defined the city, or the city defined people. Either way, Raj was uneasy about it all and wretched into his kitchen sink when he got back to Partick that night. He never saw James again and moved to Berlin shortly after. It partly prompted the drift.

In the sparse contact Raj had with Liam over the past couple of years, he got the impression James had straightened himself out now. Bought a garage in Drumry. Aff it. Taking Ashlene to the fitbaw every Saturday. In the gym. And by the looks of him in the Co-op Car Park, new teeth and new orange skin. Raj had felt a haunting shiver of anxiety outside the British Library when Liam phoned to talk about restoring Royal Enfields for a reunion. He and James were apparently selling the bikes back to the Indian market, along with other exports sent by boat, and it was proving to be some turn for them both. A rake of cash. Raj was aware of the performance of it all. Liam's civic duty to maintain turns and dealings and hang onto his ancestral "gypsy magic"; best exemplified by Liam's uncle Bunty Mac who still traded down the Barras every Saturday and once found Bobby a rare Victorian cane fly fishing rod. But even within this great pantomime of culture, Raj was still weary of James's past and penchant for vigilante justice. He was, after all those years, still relieved to part ways at the Co-op, pleasantries exchanged and a salutary wave as the HGV awkwardly manoeuvred out of the car park.

But James came back.

And here they were outside a glowing cottage with bizarre neoclassical columns under the increasingly ominous shades of the darkening sky.

James bumbled down the HGV steps and walked with ardent purpose. Bobby and Viddy hung back a bit down the dirt road. Liam and Raj had barely been able to exchange a couple of words before the oak-tiled door of the croft building widened to reveal a gaunt spectral figure in a dressing gown, backlit by candles and bearing a large bowl of Bombay mix. He held the bowl aloft and intoned:

—*Shree Ram Jai Ram Shree Ram Jai Ram. Damyata Da.*

With gentle ceremony the gaunt spectre appeared to

circle the bowl three times above his long equine head before solemnly pushing it forward towards Raj and Liam, while peering sideways at the others in some act of summoning. Or welcoming. Or blessing. Or warning.

—Good to see you again, Liam, son of Arjuna, great warrior of light! And here we are, but never really are. With the love and the light of beautiful Sita, please do come in! Preparations are complete.

The frail spectre of a man, replete with uncombed ashy hair, long bony features, and the complexion of an over-ripe monkey-nut, guided the weary procession through the oak-panelled portico and into a room that, much to Raj's awe, resembled a vault of taxiedermied tropical birds and Hindu deities. Birds, drapes, plates, sculptures, and sandalwood statues. In the brighter glow of candles, it became apparent the man was wearing a pair of those tie-dye linen trousers with "Om" signs dancing around them. The worn cloth, bobbles, and faded rainbow colours seemed like a remnant of his failed pursuit of free love and drugs in all the wrong places with all the wrong gurus. As the four of them sat – Bobby and Viddy decided to hang outside – on the large Kashan rug that covered the cold unvarnished floorboards, Raj began to imagine the man's backstory. Perhaps a recovered heroin hippie ghost from trails of old, now settled in the Highlands and Islands. They encountered a few in the Paharganj. Empty vessels, polluted veins, and a profound insistence on spiritual quests that failed them long, long ago. Raj's hunch grew stronger as the spectre folded his legs into Lotus, gently murmuring to them in an Etonian accent dampened by years of travelling with a hemp-sack full of hash and credit cards.

—Liam, baba. When we met back in Poona, you had the export plans sorted. Is all well in
   that universe?

—Aye, all is well, Bhoko-ji. We'll send a few boxes over with the bikes – kooshty.

Raj shuffled uncomfortably and arched his back with a silent sigh. He found temporary light relief in the thought that Bhoko-ji's real name was probably Jacob, or Edward, maybe Winston. Bhoko-ji, or Edward (as Raj continued to imagine him), reached for a chanter-like instrument with a bulbous upper chamber, a little like the instruments Raj had seen recently in the British Library's collection of "Orientalist" paintings. Edward blew three bending notes that blurred into one another, rising and wavering around the room like a drunk helium balloon and illuminating the beady eyes of the stuffed birds looking down on them. He placed the bulbous chanter down and spoke softly again in modulated Etonian tones.

—So. Liam, baba. What next?

—This is ma bro James, Bhoko-ji. He's gonnae take the boxes back doon the road, and we'll pack them up with the Enfields. Send those Bullets back to their spiritual home.

Edward parped three more helium-balloon notes from his bulbous chanter in some manner of applause or agreement. At this point, James was looking increasingly uncomfortable. Unable to contort his thick thighs into a Lotus position and unaccustomed to bulbous chanters and stuffed tropical birds, he appeared firmly out of his comfort zone, standing aloof in the corner of the vault. His discomfort and unfamiliarity provided gentle relief to Raj, who was continuing to survey just what the hell Liam was up to in this pantomime. He suspected, with the dread of an expectant father trying to shed old skin, they were exporting puff to India along with the bikes. He was about to find out.

Edward sprang vertical and swiftly exited into the oak-tiled hallway, appearing to shuffle past a stout old woman with a single thick grey pleat draped to her heels. He swiftly returned with two wooden boxes covered in ornate floral carvings, setting them down on the Kashan rug before gingerly tucking his heels under his thighs. Back into Lotus again. Edward leaned forward to open one of the ornately carved boxes, gurgling his throat with transcendental purpose and making rapid wiggles with his bony head. Raj palmed one side of his head and watched on with dread. He didn't want to be part of this. Edward opened the box and rejoiced gleefully. Liam ferreted down for inspection, and James continued to look like a large lost orange mammal on an alien planet. Edward opened his arms.

—And by the light of lotuses, here they are in all their splendour!

—Sound, Bhoko-ji, these are absolutely perfect! We can pack em down into the bike saddles. Pad em down for protection, eh?

With tentative courage, Raj brought himself forward to peer into the small wooden box, expecting to find compacted parcels of impending trouble. It was with a blend of relief and confusion, then, that he gazed upon colourful flashes of emerald greens, canary yellows, and ruby reds. Colourful strips of feathers bound into ornate patterns with golden hooklets and barbules. It was like a miniature painting of some tribal feathery dance as portrayed in the dream of an impressionist painter. They were beautiful. He turned to Liam.

—Fishing gear?

—Salmon flies, Raj, ma man. Gear for salmon flies. Rare gear. For fly tiers. Yi widnae believe the black market price these things go for in India, man.

—Serious?

—Serious. It's mental. Got a mate in Delhi who's got a line to the highest caste salmon fly fishers in the country. Serious money for gear like this, Raj.

—For feathers?

—It's the specific combination of feathers, man. These boys follow old Victorian recipe books. It's hard tae find any o this gear, but Bhoko-ji's time in India and his ornithology contacts... well, it's led the light for aw us. It's how we manage to fund the Enfield restorations!

—So, these guys, they pay you hundreds of pounds just for the right combination of plucked feathers?

—Thousands and thousands, mate. Thousands.

—Serious?

—Raj, mate. It's art. Antiquarian art. There was even this classical musician who broke into the British Museum of Natural History to steal exotic birds just tae get feathers like these. Punted them tae Victorian salmon tiers so he could buy a new golden flute.

—Whit?

—Aye, ano. Packed forty-seven Indian crows and ninety-eight cotingas into a wee suitcase. Punted. All for a golden flute. Mad basturt.

—Whit?

—Ano.

—Fuckin hell, man.

During this intense exchange between Raj and Liam, Bhoko-ji tried to strike up conversation with James, introducing him to a nineteenth-century guidebook to fly-tying. Recipes. Techniques. It was best to begin with one of the basic patterns like the Woolly Bugger. It was not all about patience or finger dexterity. Some of the best fly tiers had fingers like spare ribs and less patience than a Labrador. James smiled at the old Etonian hippie with a latent look of polite panic that might quickly turn to aggression. He wondered if that last comment about spare ribs might be directed at him. He'd always had hands like shovels. He wanted to make tracks, before he got himself in trouble.

—Right, boys, sorry tae rush yiz. It's just av goat Ashlene at the fitbaw the morra. Best get doon the road, eh?

Bobby bumbled into the room, delaying James's covert plea for an exit by turning towards a painting somehow bolted, or perhaps glued, to the ceiling of Bhoko-ji's ornately decorated room. None of them had noticed it until Bobby pointed up towards the image of a stern, regal, white-collared man with long sideburns and brooding brow.

—Hud on, is at nae John Nelson Darby? Boy who predicted the rapture? Faither o Dispensationalism and Futurism?

James raked his shovel hands down his face in desperation and disbelief at the situation he was in as Bhoko-ji gravitated towards Bobby, moving uncomfortably close to his head.

—Indeed it is, baba, indeed it is. And do you believe? In the rapture?

—Nae nae. Jist learned aboot it in a theology reading group ah wiz part of. Kicked me oot as I wiznae Christian. Hink I called Jesus a cult leader or summit.

—No rapture. No rising sea levels then?

—Eh?

—No nuclear war then?

—Da ken phit yer...

—Nobody worth saving at all then?

Bhoko-ji, increasingly animated, continued to unsettle James whose frustration turned to a discomfort disguised by comic quips.

—Look, lads, am aw fur a wee bit o the blood o Christ, eh! But ah really need tae get doon the road.

With the bumbling, wide-eyed help of Bobby, they packed three large boxes full of feathers, beads, and stuffed birds into the HGV. Viddy, still slouched on the stonewall dyke, shook her head in disbelief; partly at the pantomime playing out but also by the never-ending surprises of finding out who lived beside her. It could be a funny place like that. Just when it seemed she had a foot towards the lay of the land, another mound of intrigue would rise from the darkness.

James's orange dome glowed in the dark as he waved them a final farewell from the HGV as he set off down the road. Bhoko-ji shouted some prayer and closed the oak-tiled door. Raj turned to Liam.

—You're a madman.

—Just a wee turn!

—Sake.

—Right, mon team! Let's go set up camp. Am chokin fir a drink!

It was a short, jovial ride to The Storr car park, where they unbuttoned their helmets and jackets and let their loins breathe before making a decision about where to camp for the night.

THERE IS A WAR

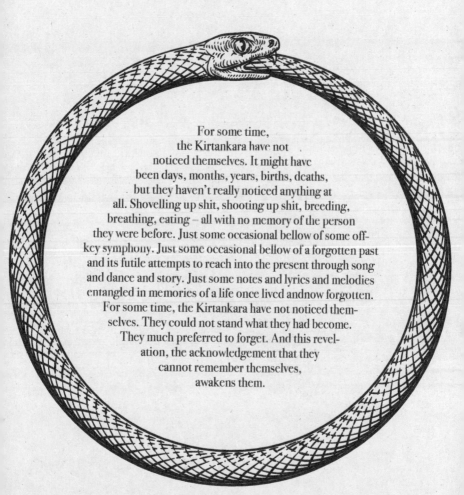

For some time,
the Kirtankara have not
noticed themselves. It might have
been days, months, years, births, deaths,
but they haven't really noticed anything at
all. Shovelling up shit, shooting up shit, breeding,
breathing, eating – all with no memory of the person
they were before. Just some occasional bellow of some off-
key symphony. Just some occasional bellow of a forgotten past
and its futile attempts to reach into the present through song
and dance and story. Just some notes and lyrics and melodies
entangled in memories of a life once lived and now forgotten.
For some time, the Kirtankara have not noticed themselves. They could not stand what they had become.
They much preferred to forget. And this revelation, the acknowledgement that they
cannot remember themselves,
awakens them.

○

Fucking posts about wild camping. Pompous hipsters in Patagonia jackets. Extendable hiking poles. Campfire selfies. Eat clean. Go light. Fuck off.

Bobby thumbed down the forum reviews while the others stretched out, bikes huddled together in a muddy corner of an overcrowded car park.

Carlos wrote:
I'm Spanish and new to Scotland, so firstly I would like to say hi to all of you writing on this forum. I am planning a 5 days trip to Isle of Skye this August and looking for some advice on wild camping in the Storr area. Are there any camp sites available in the area or any spots for wild camping with a good place to park a car within walking distance? Where can I get some decent maps of the area? Any suggestions of walks greatly appreciated too. Regards Rodrigo

An t-Eilean Sgitheanach wrote:
It's funny the amount of people who want "wild camping" within easy reach of their car! Please don't camp there, you will have to defecate and we don't want to see it. There is a campsite at Portree, on the road to Storr. Don't camp close to Storr! Stop overcrowding the site, or don't come at all!

Fucking nature Nazis. Absolute Nazis. Privileged fuckers with little else to do but police the poor, police the foreign, police all their poor fucking choices about how and where and when to camp, appreciate Skye, appreciate Scotland, appreciate nature, appreciate place. A neoliberal dominance of land in the name of conservation. Conservation for who? The same sense of entitlement that led to the price of grain rocketing up in... Bobby took a deep breath and wiped at his spectacle frames. Just let it go. Dark clouds descended, obscuring any remaining view of The Storr. No plan, place to stay, little to talk about. Liam tried to revive spirits.

—Whitya thinkin, team?

Nobody answered, so he strolled around the car park by himself sucking on a Regal. Bobby continued to thumb his phone, still straddling the back of Viddy's bike; while she and Raj stretched out at the edge of the muddy car park. Drizzle, cold, wet. The mood was damp and so were they. Raj turned to Liam.

—If there's that many cars, there's gonna be a lot of campers up there.

—True, ma man.

Viddy chimed in.

—The Storr's always this busy; should just head further north.

Bobby glanced up from his phone.

—Aye, but its dark and cal. Just find somewhere near?

The four of them muttered to one another about what might be best, light fading, necessity looming, moon blooming. Viddy wanted to avoid the nearby campsite she and John used to take the twins to and so – without revealing why – she suggested they hike a little further up The Storr path, packs on back; then go off-piste, light a fire, up tents, open a bottle. They would leave little imprint, but Bobby remained satisfied that it would still piss off the likes of *An t-Eilean Sgitheanach*. That made their shite "wild camp" all the more appealing to him. They ambled up and found a flat mossy ledge, just off the path, that would do for night. Liam popped up a tender-looking tent, two paper-thin triangles either side of a slender sleeping chamber. His black Converse were already soggy and soaked through with mud. Viddy pushed the fibreglass poles through a weather-worn four-man, while Raj and Bobby wrestled with a thick fabric that flapped loudly in the wind, struggling with a variety of worn wooden poles, all different lengths, all splintered. Raj had never seen such a thick tent cover, thinking that it more resembled a gravel sack of sorts.

—Fuck is this, min?

—Wiz Great-Granda Duthie's. Da spik ill of it, min. Been ti Dunkirk.

Raj wasn't sure if Bobby was at it, but kept quiet. He seemed sincere and serious. The tradition, the memory, the work could mean a lot to Bobby. And maybe it had been to Dunkirk. Or maybe it was important for Bobby to imagine it had been to Dunkirk.

Raj suggested lighting a fire while they unpacked, but Viddy had changed her mind and convinced them it was a bad idea. Too close to the path, and to others who might do the same and cause further erosion and litter with little care for the land. They all agreed – she made a lot more sense than that prick *An t-Eilean Sgitheanach*, Bobby thought. Relieved to have finally pitched their tents, they sat down on the damp dark ground, cold, tired, and discontented.

Reaching into the depths of his backpack, Bobby pulled out a rusty paraffin lamp.

—Vintage railway workers' lamp. Still works a treat, like. Got it up the West End a few weeks ago.

Liam looked at Bobby as if he'd pulled off some sleight of hand.

—Yi been carrying that the whole time? As well as the harmonium?

—Aye.

Bobby set the lamp down and lit it, to reveal a surprisingly pleasant golden glow that flickered across their faces in the imperfect circle they had arranged themselves in. He unpacked the harmonium and fanned it out. Puffs of air and half-notes sounded against the gentle wind. Liam reached into his sack for a bottle of Balvenie and passed it round, while Raj rescued four cans of Tennent's from the plastic seal trap customarily used for yellow can necks. Lubrication, libation, to start the conversation. Finally.

They strained to see The Storr. It was too foggy and dark now. Bobby gently droned away on the harmonium, and Raj ventured into pseudo-philosopher mode. Viddy gently rolled her eyes. Liam sparked then sucked on another Regal, as he listened to Raj's musings between sharp inhales and long exhales.

—Why do we care so much about peaks? I mean, why is The Storr, or say, climbing Ben Nevis, more popular than just immersing ourselves in landscapes? I guess it puts us in our place. The humility of decentering ourselves, shrinking ourselves to be part of larger scales of time and place.

Bobby squeezed out a low note on the harmonium, which drifted into hissy air, then silence. Raj kept talking without prompt nor reply.

—Psychogeography, man. The intertwining of self, psyche, and environment.

Bobby pulled back and the harmonium exhaled higher. Viddy fiddled with the end-tassles of her brown scarf, large eyelids and black lashes pointing down as she mumbled a response, which grew louder and more intense as it unravelled.

—I dunno. I think psychogeography is cool in the city, but out here it's all a bit... romantic? You're obsessing about your own obsession. Classic male romantic hero. The *appreciator* of nature must come to terms with his self, his psyche, his mortality in the face of the *unconquerable* wilderness that spreads out and above and around him. Such bullshit. It's like Wordsworth on shrooms at a yoga retreat for anthropo-scenesters. God, I hate that word... But anyway, have you read Nan Shepherd? I guess she gets it right when she says to walk *into* mountains instead of *up* them. We don't need to see The Storr to be in and with it. And, fuck, we don't always need to be thinking about ourselves so much.

Lids and lashes hung low, she looked a little sad to Liam, who was now blowing impressively large smoke rings, just visible in the dark. As one dispersed into nothing, he looked at Viddy.

—Shepherd sounds *groovy*, man. Defo need to check that out, *mon ami*. Pass us the whisky, eh.

Viddy's eyelids flicked up, dimpled cheeks smirking. She always found it funny when Liam used words like "groovy" and "kick stick", or dropped in French phrases like some comedic beatnik figure who sold books, black turtlenecks, bongos, and berets down the Barras on a Sunday. But he knew it was funny. It was self-deprecatory in its own way; not like Raj, who usually took himself too seriously on all matters books, music, and bongos. Liam took another swig and stubbed out his Regal on the damp grassy area beside the rock he was squatting on.

—Naw, not read Shepherd, but what yi were saying, Raj, sorta reminds me of a bit in that new Hägglund book av been reading. Like, in terms of why we go places.

His chain of thought broke as he could only think of a shite poem from a shite email. Were they his reasons? Or seasons? He pulled himself back quickly, recovered the performance.

—Listen to me saying "Like!" Like... like... bloody East-coasters. Anyway, aye, Hägglund. He goes on about how we need to focus on our finite time in existence as a way to find meaning in life. And the mountains remind of us how finite we might be, man. So mibbes yer right, Raj. It's humility.

Viddy squinted, still smirking at Liam's hepcat musings, but irked again.

—So, what, we're just supposed to sit here and think about how finite and fragile we are and be contented by that? And how does anyone have the time to even sit and do that in their daily lives? Fucksake.

Viddy thought of Adeepa and Angus, and hoped Freya had them tucked in by now. She felt guilty for being snappy in recent weeks; Freya really does mean well. Just as Viddy was dampening down to introspection, Liam caught her attention again with his rising tone.

—Aye, exactly! That's the point! We sacrifice oor lifespan to the endless appetite that capitalism has. Promotion, praise, valuation! All o that pish forsakes the hings we need most. Free time, creativity, family, joy, solidarity. Oor living time isnae spent on what brings us joy. It's just a fact. And seeing that mountain – well, the wan we can't see – helps us see that. So, in a nutshell, *mon ameees*, we aw need a new secular faith, a belief in the eternal and divine to fuck capitalism o'er and address this climate crisis, man!

Liam laughed at himself, aware of slipping into the Glasgow Uni skin he shed long ago. Back then he was all anger and anti-capitalist. Full of purpose and whisky and pints and points of view. Sticking it to the man. All performed, but fun to find it again. It felt good. Raj retorted, smiling at his old friend. Old ways, new ceremony, no small talk.

—All that sounds cool, man, but "secular faith" is a bit Dawkins, eh? It also implies that being traditionally religious is somehow at odds with caring about the planet or finding meaning in relationships. Why not just say... you have one life to live?

—I'm sure my maw has something like on her fridge, Raj.

—Aye, but does she believe it? I *know* I'm going to die. But I'm not sure I really believe it. I don't live every moment in that knowledge. Otherwise I'm not sure I'd be here with you fucking eejits!

The customary offence cut through the serious turn to mortality, before Raj finished with one final quip.

—Anyways, man, your more of a capitalist than any of us! Talk about destroying the capitalist hegemony...

—How?!

—You renovate flats, exploit students, profit from a market – and sell overpriced weed!

—Naw, mate, I've kicked that shit.

—Mate. You've two mortgages and rent out council flats bought through loans from James's garage.

—Aye, that's called helping communities when the cooncil disnae!

—You fly to ashrams in India and weird silent retreats in South America, polluting the planet.

—Pish! When was the last one I went to?

—Aye, well. What I'm saying is, it's easy to critique capitalism but forget your profits from it. Same way it's easy to rationalise mortality but forget our living moments.

—Ah suppose yiv got tae justify working for Her Majesty somehow, eh! Take the Union Jack doon Sellic Park next time we go, eh?

—Fuck off, man.

There was a bleak break in the conversation. A bitter tone had emerged. Bobby alternated between four low notes on the harmonium, meditating on the underlying tensions, nostalgia, misunderstandings, and longings between Liam and Raj that had fast condensed into one conversation. At root, Bobby thought, was Raj's frustration at Liam's continual claims of hardship, working-class credibility, and heroic social climb up the poverty-stricken ladders of the Drum. Just because his vowels burred a little harder than the others. Because the urban working class had romantic memories of unions and tenement tales. Because good ol *Glesgae* was synonymous with humble beginnings, hard childhoods, and be-ragged urchins playin fitbaw. And for all that it must surely mean Liam's meteoric rise from deprivation was a class apart from the others. Pish. For Raj, the reality was that Liam had the same opportunities as everyone else. If anything, Viddy had it more difficult growing up. Similarly, Bobby was a "first generation" (he hated the term – phit aboot the ither generations nae worth a muckle?) university student. He was well aware of his humble heritage, but there was no west coast song and Barras Ballroom jamboree about it. His family saw none of that oil money; but their vowels still didn't burr strongly enough to satisfy the west coast working class, the real working class. His school was likely less resourced than Liam's; but they didn't sing loudly enough to satisfy the friendliest people on planet Earth, who made their own city through graft and grit and unparalleled wit. None of this bothered Bobby, particularly, but he understood why Raj bristled.

Bobby pulled and pushed on the four notes, pacifying himself by thinking of "The Four Yorkshiremen" sketch, where four salt-of-the-earth Northern lads try to outdo one another's nostalgia for deprivation. Nostalgia for deprivation. What the actual fuck. What was wrong with Scottish people? And when did social class become a sought-after cultural marker as opposed to a socio-economic condition? All it does is shore up the worst parts of capitalism anyway; hard work, grit, and meritocracy being the key to success. But all's well and good when you can wave yer Saltire at graduation and say, "Kin yi believe it's happened tae a cunt like me?" Scottish people were a special kind o special. A Tennent's Super Special. Spesh as fuck, like. Spesh as fuck.

Bobby's shoulders shook into giggles, head down, hands cupped around the ivory horn, now filled with Balvenie. It broke the uncomfortable silence. Liam turned towards him.

—Fuck yi laughin at, Bobby?

—Nihin. Here. Could play a wee game.

Bobby dug around deeper into his hemp sack and pulled out what appeared to be a ragged red miniature rugby ball. He popped it out the top of the sack and it rolled awkwardly, in the way that rugby balls do, before coming to a slow, spinning stop in the middle of them. Liam was aghast.

—A fuckin rugby baw? Ah fuckin hate rugby, man.

—Nae rugby. NFL. Check eh stitches.

—Still egg chasers.

—Nah nah. Socialist sport in a capitalist country. Wage caps, ken.

—Egg chasers, man.

Raj butted in, apparently more than happy to play contrarian, especially after Liam's nibbles at him before.

—Ach rugby's not that bad. Think we've got a chip about shoulders about it up here.

Liam seemed irate.

—You shittin me, man? All that pish aboot "Ooh, we can sit together in the stands and not fight," "Ooh, we can have a pint together at the match," "Ooh, would you look at how respectful the big strappin lads are to the referee." Fuckin hate that classist pish, man, hate it. And the fact they feel the need ti constantly compare themsels tae fitbaw fans tells yi it aw. Classist wankers. Lookin down at the dregs o society.

Viddy chimed in unexpectedly.

—It's also just one big homoerotic pantomime. And God, remember those dickhead posh rugby boys at uni?

—Exactly, Viddy. Posturin, posh wankers with ideas above their station. Tories anaw. And it's shite to watch. And there's nae atmosphere at the games. And they can stick their eggs up their arse, man.

Bobby tried to calm the conversation with nuance and Doric humility. He turned to Liam.

—Well, ah suppose it's a wee bity mair complicated. Northern England has League, and it seems sounds. Fair roch, but fair.

—Ach, maybe, man. No the same up here, man. Also, whit aboot all that English egg-chasin' Empire re-enactment? "Rule Britannia", "Swing lo, Sweet Slave Driver", but it's aw awrite ciz, "Ooh, we can sit together in the stands and not fight," and it's aw aboot class, decoroum and polite manners. Pish, man. Pish. And Raj, mate, you of all people shid hate that, man!

Raj was shaking his head, looking at Liam.

—What's that supposed to mean?

—Fuck off, mate, you know whit I mean.

—You really do have a chip on your shoulder, Liam.

—Oh aye, and when did you become fuckin Gavin Hastings, defender of egg and crown? Says something about you too, mate.

Another bleak break in the conversation. Bobby wished he hadn't taken the little American football along. It was a Baltimore Ravens one he'd got while visiting the East Coast. It meant a lot to him, but it was daft to take it along, in hindsight. This was all his fault. He sighed, took a sip from the ivory horn, and began to slowly push and pull at the harmonium bellows, inhales and exhales, one breath at a time, just like his therapist had suggested. Bobby was starting to feeling drained, pale, cold, dizzied by the intensity of conversation. The paraffin lamp was still burning, but the smell was now piercing, nauseating. He patted the harmonium aside, reached into his hemp sack for the portable speaker he had brought along, syncing it to his phone, and scrolled through. The glow of the screen bent across his circular spectacles in the dark and yellow, paraffin-lit glow. They must have been there for around an hour. The Balvenie was half empty, a few cans left, seal traps safely buried at the bottom of the hemp sack. Bobby checked his saved albums and decided on Bob Dylan's *Desire*. The opening plucks of "Hurricane" emerged from the tinny speaker, followed by thumping toms, haunted fiddle, and Dylan's pistol shots firing into the night. Liam appreciated the injection of life into the increasingly lifeless night.

—Good choice, ma man! Album's class, eh.

Raj griped again. He was restless. Discontented at the discontent felt among old friends. Old ghosts he couldn't exorcise. And his frustration seeped into the conversation.

—Aye, I suppose we'll sit around pretending like some obscurity is a classic, eh.

—Whit? Obscurity?

—Aside "One More Cup of Coffee", it's all filler. Ten minutes of him screaming "Jooooeeeeyyyy" is painful; "Hurricane" lasts way too long, and the only magic in there is Emmylou, and he screwed her over too.

Bobby mustered the breath to chip in, being the biggest Dylan-nut of them all.

—I da ken, min! It's a gypsy caravan of an album, like. Fiddles, tarot cards, murderers, snakes, and ghosts. Nae muckle like it.

—Aye, and you're the authority are yi, Bobby?

Bobby sulked back against his harmonium, exhausted. Viddy squeezed the centre of her forehead between thumb and index finger, large eyelids pointing down in a frown, angry at Raj for shouting Bobby down. He shouldn't do that. Not with his fragilities. She had to say something.

—Why does Dylan always have to be such a bro-off? Guys LOVE to bond and argue and outdo each other's Bobness. Why? The mythology? Some crush over femininity channelled into a folk troubadour that straight dudes can secretly crush over without feeling too emasculated? Also, what about the way he treated Emmylou, or Joan? Or the erotic fantasy of CHEATING with "Johanna". It's nostalgia for a folk patriarchy that was never all that in the first place. It's fucking boring. And I'm cold. We should just go to sleep.

—Aye, okay, chill out, Viddy.

—Fuck off, Raj. You're the one being a wee prick, as usual. Subtly provoking people, all gentle jibes and intellectual snobbery. I haven't missed this at all.

—Nobody's provoked, Viddy. It's not my fault if folk can't have a conversation about music...

—You're such a dick sometimes.

—Sometimes? Yiv not seen anyone in years! How would you even know?

A sombre silence fell between them as the music was fast drowned out by rumbles of wind and the smatter of rainfall on their waterproofs. It was getting colder, wetter, and nobody wanted to talk. Viddy was now huddling into her own knees, head down, straggles of black hair slithering from a damp hood onto waterproof trousers. Bobby rocked back and forth with his harmonium case in some attempt to generate heat in the darkness, whilst Raj shivered and shook his head, then shivered some more. Liam roused himself to adopt the ironic role of morale-boosting peacekeeper.

—Sake, boys and girls. Whit a night, eh! Pity we don't have a wee Carlos Vally. Keep the spirits up … or down, mibbes.

Raj couldn't be bothered with the performance.

—I dunno, it just seems pointless. We're cold, can't have a fire, probably sitting on sheep shite, pretending like we are some beatnik biker gang when we're actually too old for this shit. What the fuck we even doing here?

—Touchy, eh, Raj.

—Aye, *we've* all grown up, Liam.

—Fuck's that supposed to mean?

—We're not nineteen, twenty, whatever you were back then. Life's moved on.

—Nervous much, big man, eh?

—About what?

—Yer borin fuckin life and all yid wish yi had done.

—You're a loser, Liam. Maybe yi always were.

—Fuckin watch it, ma man, watch it.

—Aye, that's it, eh. Intimidate us all with your fake tales of prison and hardship and… ach, fuck it, man.

Liam's red mist began to rise, eyes widening. Raj felt a pang of fear. He remembered the unrestrained rage that lay beneath the brashness, the insecurities. The pizza. Bobby's teeth. The Gallowgate. Hammers. That old American hippie in the Paharganj who scratched around Liam's past long enough to make him bite. Raj remembered how the American hippie introduced himself as Dood, spelling out the letters "D-o-o-d" as he pulled at his red-and-white handlebar moustache and damped at an orange headband between rolling cigarettes and downing Kingfishers. Three Kingfishers down, Dood began to make passes at Viddy before awkwardly asking Raj if she was "his girl or not". The audacity of ownership. Four Kingfishers down, Dood unleashed a diatribe about how India was headed for capitalistic disaster. The tourism of hypocrisy. Five Kingfishers down, Dood began to rile Liam. The performance of violence past.

—I dunno, man. You guys are motely, man. Liam, aint you too old for this shit?

—Whit?

—"Whit!" It's funny the way you say that, man. Ooh. WHIT! Mad intimidating.

—Whit yi gettin at, Dood?

—I'm shittin you, man. You just seem older than these guys.

—Aye, well, we're mates at uni, y'know. No that different, eh.

—Yeh, man. You just don't seem the type. I don't meet guys like you too often on the road, y'know?

—Whit's the "type"? Whit yi gettin at, Dood?

—Like, these guys are probably all blissed out in some youthful year on the road or something. Worrying their parents, pleasing themselves, blah blah blah – it's a tired and boring old story. But you. Your type don't usually even leave home.

At the utterance of "leave home" Liam shot up and smashed a half-empty bottle of Kingfisher against the wall opposite from where Dood was gesticulating with his joint. Grasping for a small stool, Liam launched it with one swift underarm swoop, sending it crashing and splintering into four pieces beside Dood, who was now wide-eyed and frozen with fear. For about a minute that felt like ten, Liam spat vitriol and violence from the safe distance of the opposite wall of the hostel lounge area. Bobby curled up in a corner, covering his head, tapping his fingers together nervously. Raj and Viddy got between Liam and Dood, in the manner of two boxing referees trying to shoo a scurrying pitbull from beneath the knees of a placid opposing fighter. Dood left after a few apologetic pleas, clasped hands, quivering knees. Flaring down, Liam lit a cigarette and frowned, breathed heavy, then frowned some more. Dood must have thought he was some caricature. Maybe he was. And he just proved it anaw. Fuck it. He could never really escape "home" or himself. Fuck it. Bobby wondered if the whole affair might have merely been an issue of accent. Burrs and vowels romantically known for a violence that provoked the performance of a violence. But maybe he was overthinking it. Either way, the four of them were shaken into an intimacy that night, finding comfort in one another rather than within themselves.

It was different now, though. Raj knew he had overstepped. He'd purposefully trod on a wound that could never heal. He dreaded what was coming as Liam shot up, mumbling and grumbling and fumbling in anger; but then he unexpectedly circled past Raj entirely, taking on a worried tone.

—Fuck's that cunt doing?

Bobby had left the circle and was ambling down the muddy path to the car park, mumbling something to himself. The others looked to each other, concerned, realising they hadn't spoken to him much, if at all. Liam shouted after him.

—Here, Bobby! Yuptae, fucksake?!

Bobby, pirouetted. Then pirouetted again. Then stopped. They could make out a wobbling silhouette, but little else. His voice, broken to a higher pitch than usual, screamed out in his wilderness.

—This is makin me nervous. And talk *tooo* me! Da talk aboot me!

—We werenae talkin about yi, Bobby, mon back!

—D'yi think I'm deed? Some good stories to be had, eh. Good een.

Raj sighed, threw a worried glance towards Liam. Bobby wasn't right. Meanwhile, Viddy looked increasingly worried too. She spoke in a more panicked tone than befitted her typically measured self.

—What should we do? I can't handle another one. I just can't.

Viddy quivered in the darkening night, hands clawing at her face. It wasn't clear what she was referring to. Death? John? Bobby? What came before? What was yet to come? The others freeze-framed in the dim murmur of rusty lamplight. It was like they had been there before. They saw something, no, felt something, from the past. A zooming out, or winding back, or lifting up above the black soggy Storr. There he was, Bobby, panicking his way through the porticos of a snaking imperial train clanking its way towards Amritsar. Alone, hyperventilating, and pushing his way past a stern Sikh man and bony laughing child and clanging at the chai-wallah's steel pots just before the frothy brown liquid treacled down towards the conflict. The conflict which he was running from. The conflict he was trying to prevent, unbeknown to the combatants in all their fire and fury and flame. Now, the combatants stood here. In the darkening night. No longer entangled and tumbling in satchels and arguments but rather per-plexed by what they might have missed or prevented. This collective feeling, this unspoken remembrance of a past event, seemed to upend any notion of their own personal memories and unite them in that moment. It rendered themselves obsolete as they submitted to the fiction of a shared past. Viddy wiped at her brows as if to wake herself from a dark and deepening reverie, bound for nowhere but a murky ocean-bed of decay.

—We have to go find him. Seriously. It's Bobby. I should have seen this coming too!

Raj tried to reassure her, shuffling around in the wind.

—Don't worry, Viddy, it's not you. I just think he's having a bad moment. Give him a few minutes. I'll head down there and... fuck!

The three shot up as the erratic revs of a motorcycle thundered down the road, reverberating around the Storr. Liam accidently kicked over the rusty lamp, shrouding them in a darkness as he cried out.

—Tell me you yi didn't give him the bike keys, Viddy?!

—I left them in the bike! I remembered a few minutes ago but I was too cold to move. It's Skye! Nobody is gonna get that far on an old Enfield!

—Bobby cannae ride for toffee, man! Remember the fuckin goat! And it's dark!

The revs grew louder, more erratic, more distant. Liam bolted down the dirt path, while Raj and Liam scrambled to pack up Bobby's lamp, harmonium, and hemp sack. Through the luck of their own incompetency, the tents were easily packed and hoisted over shoulders. The bags rattled as Raj and Viddy followed Liam towards the car park, ambling and tripping their way down in the dark. Liam took command, Raj exhaled anxiously. Viddy pinched harder between her eyes.

—Right, Viddy, jump on the back of Raj's bike, eh? I'll race ahead and do a reccy.

—No, Liam. I'll ride up ahead, let me go.

—Sake, just go with Raj. It's not the time.

—What? Liam! I'm the only one who can actually ride, and I live on Skye! You take Raj and let me go!

Raj tried to move things along, anxious as to Bobby's whereabouts.

—Here, Viddy, just take my keys. I'll ride with you, and we can follow Liam. Come on, we need to find Bobby. He's not right.

—Fine. Careful, Liam, these roads are no joke in the dark.

—Aye. That's why we need to find Bobby.

And they drifted into the dark night.

A MOTORCYCLIST MUST DIE

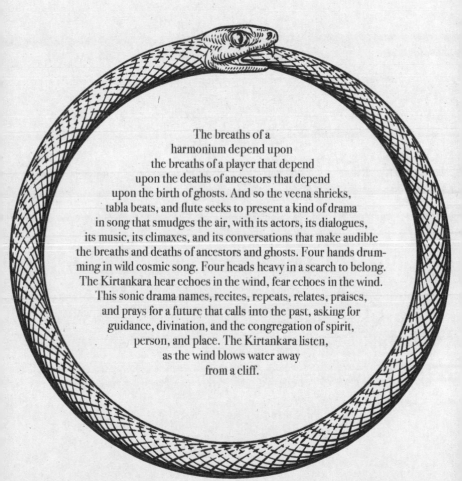

The breaths of a
harmonium depend upon
the breaths of a player that depend
upon the deaths of ancestors that depend
upon the birth of ghosts. And so the veena shrieks,
tabla beats, and flute seeks to present a kind of drama
in song that smudges the air, with its actors, its dialogues,
its music, its climaxes, and its conversations that make audible
the breaths and deaths of ancestors and ghosts. Four hands drumming in wild cosmic song. Four heads heavy in a search to belong.
The Kirtankara hear echoes in the wind, fear echoes in the wind.
This sonic drama names, recites, repeats, relates, praises,
and prays for a future that calls into the past, asking for
guidance, divination, and the congregation of spirit,
person, and place. The Kirtankara listen,
as the wind blows water away
from a cliff.

○

Bobby was angry and scared at what he believed they had become. From the novel viewpoint of the bike, he thought he saw a yellow fish ripple across the dark loch that seemed to stretch for miles between symmetrical mountains rising down to the water and up to the sky. An internal monologue whispered inside of himself, or maybe outside. It was hard to tell. Too much talk, too little compassion, too many dead selves around an unlit fire with nae muckle embers. Time spent arguing was time lost forever. Best to take a moment, leave them to it, breathe, come back to nothing special, situation was kind of nervous, best to take a moment, leave them to it, come back to nothing special. Bonnie stars the nicht, and the licht of the loch is a halo. Chill oot. The problem with exercising free will is that it's niver withoot ramifications and therefore nae really "free" or "wilful" at all. Ach, will see them later or imorn. Wasting time that would be lost forever. Dead selves around an unlit fire with no embers, ken.

Pangs of guilt fell into facial squints in the darkness of night as Bobby thought of the worry he might have caused the others by leaving. It was a feeling he had become accustomed to over the past few years; the need to look after himself was always complicated by the impact his methods of self-preservation had on others. It was partly why he'd found it so hard to open up. It led to quiet introversion, which had its merits. He was able to focus more on therapy, magic tricks, and settling into dusty brown bean cushion bliss. But all that came at the cost of wondering how others saw him. The worry, the questions, the stigma. They probably preferred the gentleman he was before. Jovial. Jaunty. The loveable eccentric. Dead selves.

It was about a year or so after finishing his PhD that the newly titled Dr Robert Milne was born into one of the worst days of his life. No job security, balding, a bad break-up; there were tangible factors to why he was feeling low, which he did acknowledge whilst sinking solo pints in silence after teaching undergraduate tutorials that just about covered the cost of rent. But he could never have seen, in that virgin sense of self, what was coming.

Granda Duthie had long been a keeper of Scottish Terriers, or Aiberdeen Terriers, as he preferred to call them, and was, in fact, twice president elect of the Scottish Terrier Club of Aberdeenshire. The dogs were also known as "diehards" due to their endless grit and determination, and Bobby was raised on Granda Duthie's tales about the breed – swashbuckling adventures against the English; badger herding; and an unfortunate susceptibility to craniomandibular osteopathy. Granda Duthie's aging Aiberdeen Terrier, Dinkle, had been a friend to Bobby for a good seven years but also happened to trigger the outbreak, which began on a summer visit to Oldmeldrum in the summer of 2012.

On a rare and stifling hot Aberdeenshire day, foreheeds dripping like knackered fridge-freezers, Granda Duthie caned his way through to the council house kitchen to pour two glasses of lemonade and ice for the loons. As Bobby sat damp and humid in a sorry state of contemplation about his break-up and bad financial state, Dinkle, with an apparent empathetic sixth sense, lay his head over Bobby's lap, and swished his tongue up his inner thigh, which was protruding from the baggy combat shorts chosen especially for the weather. Later that evening, on a glowing sunset Scotrail train back down to Glasgow, the Stonehaven coast glistening to his left, Bobby fell victim to the horror. The sheer horror. The sincere realisation that he might have enjoyed it when Dinkle licked his thigh. For three more hours and up until arrival at Queen Street station, Bobby was trapped in a terrifying state of rumination. Was it sexual? Was it because he was lonely? Did a dog do something to him when he was a child? How could he be so disgusting? So bestial?

And so began a prolonged period of internal turmoil in which Bobby violently tortured himself – or, as he would later learn, *it* tortured him. He wouldn't walk to the shops as there might be someone walking a dog. The television was out of bounds in case a nature documentary proved arousing. Was it arousing? He put on a *Planet Earth* DVD to "check" and was horrified to find goosebumps pop up over his arms. His body was reacting to the thoughts, which meant they must be real. He looked at old pictures of himself with childhood pets and was paralytic with fear and mentally revisited every possible moment, looking for clues. It was agony. The constant self-questioning. Was he too close to animals as a child? Did he accidently touch Granda Duthie's dogs inappropriately? Did other people see him looking at animals like this? Was he a freak to everyone and he just didn't know?

After a year of online shopping, little television, social isolation, and continually recasting past narratives about himself in relation to animals, sex, arousal, and bestial monstrosity, Bobby finally submitted, in a helpless release of pain and tears and self-loathing, to telling his mum. It was the hardest thing he had ever done. He was so ashamed of who he had become. So disgusted. She would surely prefer the gentleman he was before. Yet with the wit, strength, compassion, and perceptive understanding of a mother unrepentantly bound to loving her son, Moira found a way. She made Bobby laugh again, arranged for therapy, and was the first to suggest, to Bobby's initial scepticism and denial, that it might be a form of OCD she'd heard about during her nursing days.

Blessed with the care of one particularly experienced therapist in Queen Margaret's, Bobby learned about Pure O – "purely obsessional" – about checking, ruminating, mental compulsions, and the need for certainty. He learned about harmful misunderstandings where sufferers were wrongly advised to seek out sex therapy. He learned it was a disorder of anxiety and uncertainty, not sexual urges and behaviours. He learned that the primitive worry-brain could randomly select a theme – in his case, bestiality – that feels like it needs to be resolved immediately through compulsions. He learned to identify his Pure O as "it" – an "it" apart from him-self. He began to think of "it" as an angry octopus which had appeared at a stressful time in his life, lathering and tightening its tentacles around all aspects of his brain and being, squeezing him into submission. He began to make peace with the octopus, inviting it to do its worst. He came to learn about exposure and response. He began to expose himself, with the help of his therapist, to animal pictures. He intentionally walked to the shop, knowing he might pass a dog and recognise an intrusive thought. He went to public parks, and watched *Planet Earth* again, all the while imagining the octopus wriggling around and waiting for one of its tentacles to inaugurate a thought.

These were the great liberations he found through intensive CBT, through Queen Margaret's, and if they wanted to call it a "lunatic asylum", so be it. The liberations had granted him a new strength, and it had been no easy journey to get to that point. He remembered one of the first therapists he saw, a bespectacled male psychoanalyst, who initially helped him prise open and identify past behaviours, before sending him spinning further into chaos. When Bobby was fifteen, he watched, unbeknown to his mum, the film *Dead Man Walking* and felt what can only be described as fear and horror at the sexual assault scene in the woods. Every night after that, for the following year, he *had* to touch a poster in his room ten times with his fingers crossed. For if he didn't, maybe it could happen to his mother. Even thinking of the film and the poster and the fear years later would induce shudders, and sometimes even a physical paralysis. The bespectacled psychoanalyst helped him understands this was also clearly an early outbreak of obsessive thinking, though it had gone unrecognised, or undiagnosed. But the therapist took a harmful turn.

—And you see, Bobby, this just shows that you have suffered with obsessive and compulsive behaviours throughout your life. And it's quite normal that the first outbreak occurs in boys around puberty.

—Aye. Had nae idea what it was at the time. See it noo, like. That feeling. That thinking reoccurring in different ways at different times, like.

—Do you see any common factors, though, Bobby? Across these different outbreaks and episodes?

—Well, I get paralysed by my thoughts every time. It's excruciating.

—Okay, but what about the sexual nature of the outbreaks? And the fact it starts with your mother?

And with that question, and in that moment, the room and the therapist and Bobby's heart sank into a dark pit of fear as he began to revisit, again, every moment in every episode. His mother; sexual assault; Viddy's assailant on the train; sex with animals; sex; sex; sex. Oh fuck, he was clearly fucked up and obsessed and bestial and Freudian and fucked up and... he left the psychoanalyst's office hyperventilating and worse off than when he arrived.

But after his liberation at Queen Margaret's, Bobby realised that OCD, the multi-tentacled octopus in his head, simply attacked the things he loved the most. His love for his mother, who was doing her best to raise him as a single parent. His love for animals, and particularly Granda Duthie's "diehard" Dinkle. His love for his friends, particularly Raj, Viddy, and Liam. If the octopus wanted to arm an attack using sex and sexuality, it was merely utilising a meaningless weapon. It had, he discovered, little to do with his psyche or childhood trauma or anything buried within that needed to surface. And even if there were things buried within, he need not worry about them, as he knew that they too could or would be weaponised into intrusive thinking by the octopus. Stinking thinking. Analysis paralysis. Recognising these patterns retrospectively, and in the present, was like throwing off shackles. Throwing off tentacles. A liberation.

Aye, Bobby thought. He *had* come a long way. Was in a good place now. Little did any of them know. Little do any of us know. They had probably been through shit too. Poor Viddy. She must've had it worst, with her family forced away fae Sri Lanka and all. Little do we know. A lot happens in a few years. No point in arguing. Would be time wasted. Little do we often know.

With a sudden jolt caused by a pothole in the road, Bobby woke from his wide-eyed reverie to remember he was at the helm of an unwieldy screaming machine he had little control of. The simultaneous sensation of movement and stillness effected a oneness that was as terrifying as it was invigorating. The Bullet's sublime. The first therapist Bobby saw for OCD had asked him to take morning runs and monitor his thoughts in terms of content and anxiety levels, which he would then rate on a scale of one to ten before and after the run. Amidst the clamping tentacles of intrusive thoughts, Bobby became increasingly mindful of the relationship between his mind and body. Sometimes his legs would be moving, beating down on the road, but his mind had given up. He went back to thinking wild octopus thoughts. He couldn't go on. But he went on. Other times his mind would tell him he could run for ten more minutes, but his legs ceased to carry out the endeavour. He struggled to align the two. The mind. The body. Their separation. It was a relationship that was dysfunctional, lagging, and in need of a few candlelit dinners and conversations about all they once were before things got bad. It was also why motorcycle travel was so disconcertingly thrilling. Still *and* moving. Body and mind forced to come to terms with it all. The Bullet's sublime.

Having not moved from second gear throughout his evening escapade, Bobby shakily sputtered towards a left-hand turn in the road, signposted for Elishader. It could be a good place to camp out, easy for them to find in the morning. Surely they wouldn't bother looking for him tonight. And he was an adult, fucksake. Be fine. See out the night with the spare bivvy he'd packed as an alternative to Granda Duthie's Dunkirk tent, which would take too long to put up in the dark anyway. A night under the stars. There might be sheep around, but he was fine with that now. He smiled.

Ditching the bike and unfurling his bivvy bag under a dark blanket of glistening sky, Bobby sat back peacefully but found himself unable to sleep. They *would* be worried. Such was the way of things for those with the label of being mentally fragile. Others would always worry. Often needlessly. It hadn't always been like that. He thought back to India; how he was probably seen as the wise one. Bardic, quirky, clever, eccentric. Harmonium, horn-rimmed glasses, books, blunts. Loveable, eccentric genius. Yet none of those things were true. Sure, when in a prosperous chapter of his life, he was the jovial big loon with confidence and fly style. But when times got hard, those very things rendered him the unhinged eccentric that was prone to falling off a cliff. Bobby began to doubt himself, doubt his past. They probably didn't even think of him as the big jovial loon at all anyway. He thought of the panic attack he had. On the train. It was the octopus getting the better of him, but all that was hindsight, and what did hindsight matter now? He should have just got drunk on the Sikh's whisky and eaten Fazrudin's aloo tikki, but nah, big fragile Bobby had to go and freak out when everyone else was having fun. Old horn-rimmed Doc Tattie would always be prone to worrying others; and that itself was too much to bear in the darkness. No matter how cool or funny or bright he might have been in the light. That was the reality of stigmatization. The persistent and problematic conflation of eccentricity and creativity with mental illness. Bobby thought of Elton John. He could be all *Rocketman*-cool with big feather boas one moment, but then the drugged out "gay guy" with Daddy issues the next. God knows it was surely too much for people to appreciate that there didn't need to be a connection between the two. Normalcy. That poisonous and unavoidable construct. It was hard to know how to be. It was hard to know who to be. Bobby remembered reading about the etymology of eccentric. It apparently derived from the Greek *ekkentros* – an astronomical term denoting a circle from which the Earth, sun, or another object deviates, from a central point. He imagined himself from a telescopic, vertical viewpoint as he gazed up at the stars, peripheral and scattered under a darkening blanket. He exhaled, remembered to breathe. It had been a long day. Things were fine. He'd catch up with them in the morning.

But Bobby was unable to sleep.

So, he went for a walk in his own dark wilderness.

The two Royal Enfield Bullets rattled up the dark bowels of an island long acquainted with midnight rovers and ramblers. Third eye shining, the circular headlamp of Viddy's bike beamed over concrete, hillside, and ditch. Searching. The pale red dot of Liam's screeching rear light refracted through her helmet visor. She drifted in and out of darkness, the meandering roads turning from black to bright to shades of crimson, then back to black. Viddy had lost track of how long they'd been riding, and where they might be. Everything felt panicked and rushed when they left the The Storr car park, bodies like searchlights. But on the road, the sense of moment, seconds, minutes, memories had become evasive, stalled by the search for someone in crisis. Looking for Bobby had become an uninterrupted succession of turns, revs, bleak visions, and black spots. She knew they were somewhere up the A855, cutting through veins of living water, but was unsure where. The air smudged into song, the night was thick. They could have been anywhere.

Raj, riding pillion, felt the cotton edges of his helmet moist with teardrops, which flowed unexpectedly. Somehow, in this moment of panic and crisis, he felt more alive, nostalgic, sentient, human. It was strange how tragedy, or the looming sense or possibility of it, could light the wick of something inside himself he'd forgotten. Maybe Bobby was there to remind of him that, but he was gone now. They were here now. They would turn a corner again soon, and surely find Bobby with a doob and stoic groan about what they were doing riding around at night.

Viddy continued to glimpse flashes of Liam's circular crimson light as it ghosted around bends in the road. She thought of putting the twins to bed at night, and how they could only sleep if they knew she was in the dimly lit room, turtle lullabies chiming. They didn't need to be touched, nor spoken to, nor seen, but needed her presence. Her ghostly presence. If she left the room, quietly as possible, they would scream rabidly into a void of loss and loneliness which prevented them from balance, from sleep. Perhaps we never quite shed the skin of the child inside of us. She watched the crimson blur to black and back again every few seconds and thought further. We need the subliminal presence to air around us, even though we pretend we can't see them, until they are gone.

Up ahead, Liam slowed, his pale red dot brightening from a blurry shape to a fully formed circle. Viddy dropped down to second, engine protesting, then first, engine screaming, then flexed her left toes to bring the machine, souls, and some particles of time, to a halt. It jolted Raj out of melancholic reverie. He had been stationary in movement, but now he was just stationary, behind an old friend he'd not seen in a while and had been a prick to in the cold depths of a pointless night around a paraffin lamp. Liam stopped by the roadside, third eye shining, but his typically commanding glance had turned to one of loss and incompetence; failure disguised by aggression, burrowed brow, frown.

—Fuck knows where the mad basturt's gone. Whitdiyae wanna dae?

Viddy sighed.

—We should keep searching.

—Searching for whit?! We could be riding around in the dark all night, man.

—He's probably just gone up the coast a bit. Am sure we'll catch up.

A microsecond later, or maybe it was much more, Viddy looked around and realised where Liam had stopped. Just outside Elishader. They were close to the car park behind Mealt Falls. The flap of Kilt Rock was blowing in the bleak dark beyond. Liam wrenched his left thigh up over the bike and turned to face Viddy and Raj, who were both still, silent, and stationary over the bike.

—Let's just get some kip somewhere near, eh? We need tae sleep. Bobby'll be okay. Boy can look after hisel.

The wind rattled and crackled against their waterproofs. Viddy and Raj dismounted and stumbled against each other as the bike tilted sideways. They unbuttoned their helmets to regroup. It was the closest they had felt to one another in a long time. The shake of Viddy's thick, damp, black hair reminded him of another time; and the touch of Raj's body was some forgotten comfort to her. Viddy collected her thoughts, brown scarf flapping against her cheeks, rain threatening, urging them to find a hole to burrow in for the night. She composed herself.

—If we carry on for a couple of minutes, we should come to a narrow access road. We can leave the bikes there and set up camp just behind Mealt Falls. There's a flat bit of ground between the car cark and cliff fence that should be solid enough for the tents. Time is it, anyway? How long's Bobby been away?

Liam guessed they had been on the road for about twenty minutes, bodies like searchlights. Perhaps it was the plight of their situation, but Viddy felt disorientated by Liam's response. She knew it was a short distance from The Storr to Elishader, but it felt like they had been riding around for hours. If only the blooms of the people and landscapes around her were as linear in her mind as they were on all the tourist signs that showed timelines of dinosaur remains and Jurassic rocks. The timepiece of mind would have to wait – it was getting darker, wetter. They carried on up the A855 for a few minutes, or some undefinable time.

The Royal Enfield Bullets jolted around erratically, pulling them over and around loose rocks on the access road, first gear functioning like a winch towards some predestination. Glancing up to her left, Viddy noticed a red and white sign, or perhaps it just looked red and white. The rear eye of Liam's Enfield was beaming back against her own headlamp, and it was hard to tell. She squinted at the streaks refracting through her visor and tried to focus, allowing the blurs to formulate shapes, signifiers, and signs that might become comprehensible as she and Raj continued to be thrown against each other, then forced apart by fragments of rocks on the road. She deciphered the outline of a figure in the middle of the red rectangle, falling backwards, head-first, something protruding from his back. Around the figure were jagged shapes, ice-like fragments that appeared to be melting into a singular, squiggly line which ran the length of the bottom edge of the rectangle. The bike pulled itself closer to the sign, and Viddy felt both arms abruptly dragged to the right, having to quickly pull back on the handlebars in order to right herself. The white shapes at the top of the triangle became clearer, bolder.

Cliffs,
please
take care!

The text was not transparent. Why was the comma there? And why was there a line break between "Cliffs" and "please"? To whom was the subject? The plea? The same person who had to, "take care!"? Or someone else? How the fuck were we supposed to know who...

Raj spoke up.

—Y'alright, Vid? You've been quiet since we left The Storr.

—Hard to talk when you're riding, Raj, but yeh, am okay. Just tired. Overthinking. S'alright. Just overthinking, eh. Let's just set up and get some rest for a bit. We're almost there.

Liam's bike swung a gentle right towards the coast, off the veiny access road and into the car park, an eyelet in the rock face. He braked abruptly, engine fading down to the whistle of wind, and Viddy pulled up beside him, parallel, in line, looking forward. They bowed their heads in quiet trepidation at what they saw before them.

It was Bobby's bike, cast onto its side, displaced, bags strewn and bleeding out of the back seat.

They were there now – but he was gone.

Nowhere to be seen.

They felt unknowing, nowhere, all nowhere gone, and watched the wind blow the water away from the cliff, never reaching the bottom, blowing into nothing.

I TRIED TO LEAVE YOU

Nothingness is never nothing,
not even when the Kirtankara believe
it to be so. For where one sees a long cont-
inuum, another sees cycles, and still another
sees time in oscillation. And in art, and in song,
and in dance, they differ too. Some try to leave. Close
the book. Others try to awaken old selves every morning.
The Koodiyattam of Kerala count microseconds as trillions
of years. Thus, death and dancing and songs all echo beyond
nothingness; in the wind, in lungs, in organs, in notes,
in hearts, in harps, and in the wind. It's better in the
wind when a flautist pipes the melody. It's better
in the wind when the Kirtankara listen
for the notes. It's better in the wind.
It's better in the wind.

○

With gentle ceremony, columns of light began to form on the inside of the tent Raj and Viddy had shared for a sleepless few hours, bodies curled in opposite corners, awkward and writhing with worry. Viddy pulled down the internal zip, causing an abrasive scraping sound which stirred Raj. He sat up gingerly, sleeping bag coiled around his midriff. Outside of the tent, Liam was walking around in the same clothes he had on the night before. Perhaps he hadn't slept. Likely looking for Bobby, certainly looking lost. He appeared as shivery and fragile as the others felt.

They conversed sparsely, tried to formulate a plan, and wondered about calling the police whilst repeatedly trying Bobby's phone. They were, Raj thought, in some kind of second state of consciousness, maybe even ecstasy. Their minds were removed from regular function; bodies displaced, detached, fragile, sensitive, paranoid, scared – but also somehow elated. It was an intensity of experience none of them had felt in a while. Viddy squatted, raked hands through her hair, and began a great trance. Liam narrated what he thought were the facts, trying to get a firmer foothold on the situation, the lay of the land.

—No signs he took anything from the bike. He's either gone off on foot or...

The rest of the words did not need said. Sometimes language was like that. He changed the subject.

—Ahve got some wee coffee sachets. Will get the gas stove

on and may as well have another scoop on the bikes after. If we call anyone now, it's just gonnae be panic stations.

The three of them squatted in silence, sipping coffee, cliffs below, heads low, staring at the grassy earth below their feet. It was damp, smudging, dissolving; entropic. The water continued to gush from the edge of the cliff. Droplets dispersed from one another, blowing away into nothing. The night had bled into day; or perhaps day into night. The light had dimmed for a brief moment before birdsong, but now there were faint ribbons of yellow sun. The sea brightened, the planet glowed from above and below. A quiet peace fell upon them in all their internal toil. Their sleepless haze left no room for performed manners, polity, or greetings. The coffee tasted like a cocktail of tin and talcum powder. Residue singed and soured their tongues, causing Liam to swish the remaining liquid around like a morning mouthwash, before he set off back to the car park to see if Bobby had taken anything else from the bike. It had been a cold night. Too cold to sleep out. Raj and Viddy creaked up from their squatted silence, knocking back their tin-talc coffee, and opting to amble along the uneven field of faint greens that kissed the lapping coast. Their footsteps, breath, and conversation were slow, carefully placed, almost meditative. Raj broke the morning silence with a sincere tone at once concerned and unpanicked. The numb voice of an early morning or late night.

—This is fucked up, man. Not what I expected.

—Things rarely are.

—True.

The wind blew harder, threatening a fiercer turn, before dampening down to allow the lapping waves and waterfall to echo across the faint green field.

—Think he's just checked into a B&B somewhere?

—Doubt it. Island's pretty much dead that time of night.

—How's that been?

—What?

—Dunno. Life here. Or the lack of it. Big change from gigs in Glasgow, hog-farming in Landes... all the places you hopped around after uni.

The spluttering cackles of sheep reverberated in and around the hollow coastal wind.

—It's never felt empty.

—I get what you mean. Guess it's full on with the twins as well.

—Not really full on. Just a fragile place to be in. The most intense blend of love and tiredness and fear. Can leave you... I dunno, just fragile. Hard to know how to stay strong for them sometimes.

—How you been doing, Viddy? Since the accident?

—Fuckin fantastic. Nah, I mean... Hollow. Alone. But also, weirdly okay. I don't want to leave here. There's nothing I need to escape. John would love to see me, see us, keep the croft. I'm just sacred that I'm forgetting him already. Or more that I'm ready to forget him. Kinda want to forget him.

The waves seemed to ripple a calm gold as Viddy stopped for a moment, eyes swimming and swirling and tossing themselves around in sadness.

—You're strong, Viddy. I dunno how you do it.

—You'll be fine, Raj.

—Eh?

—You'll be fine too. You'll be a good dad. I always saw that in you.

—Really?

—Yeh. Actually, remember when we all got high in McLeod Ganj with mad Samir and that Belgian sax player in the little cabin? Liam was on one of them highs where he couldn't stop talking, but I remember looking at you and slipping into this weird vision. I imagined your face older, wrinkled, eyes and voice weathered by the weight of time. I saw you walking through this field with three white horses, holding the hand of a little girl in blue jeans with big brown curls puffing over her shoulders. It was beautiful and I knew then you would be a great dad. Three white horses and a little wee girl grasping at your hand with the tenderness of unconditional love. It was like a memory of the future.

—Why didn't you tell me?

—I was high as hell, Raj! Think I ended up going to bed. Liam and Samir were also doing my nut in, talking so much. And I was probably freaked out by even thinking about kids back then.

—Yeh. Guess I'm still freaking out a bit. Feels like a part of me is going to die.

—It will. But another part will be born. It's like shedding old skin for the better of your body. And your mind. Your whole being, really.

—Just feel too much of a mess. Too much of a child myself! If I'm all mixed up, she could be ten times worse. She'll be lost. I'm still lost.

—And so what if she is? She'll find her own songs to figure all that out. And it might be beautiful. Things were alright for us in the end.

—Were they? Are they?

—Yeh, they are.

—Aye. Spose they are.

The wind rattled and rasped at the thin tarpaulin fabric beside them, before fading to a whirling sound just soft enough to allow Raj to speak again.

—Vids? Did you ever think about us? Like, how things might have been?

—Jesus, Raj. Course. Doesn't everyone? I get weirded out by other people who kill old loves. Like they never existed. Like it's the best thing to never reflect. Fuckin weird man.

—Love? Do you think it was that?

—Nah, but we had our special moment.

—Aye, we did. Why do you think it didn't work?

—Jesus, I dunno. We were young. It was just a fling. I wasn't ready. And...

Viddy paused, casting her eyes downwards in a manner that suggested she didn't want to hurt Raj by saying anymore. But the sincerity of his eyes prompted her to continue.

—I always felt you were looking for an ally in me. Like we should have some inherent bond just because of where our parents were from and how *British* they felt and how weird that was for us. I just wasn't interested. I wanted something else. You wanted to dwell and discover and uncoil colonial snakes with me, but it was too tiring. I needed something else.

—Aye. You processed all that stuff a lot quicker than me. It's different now. I've come to terms with... I dunno what to call it, personal coloniality?

—What's that? Some new in-word?

—Nah, I dunno. It's like families, relationships, loves. All these things indirectly fractured by a political past we had no control over. Before, I couldn't understand how my dad could go from a family of oppressed Vaishyas to praising Queen and country! But I get it now. Now that it's too late. Too fractured.

The wind spluttered damp specks of rain across their waterproofs as a sad silence fell upon them. Raj continued to cathartically lament. He told Viddy about his recent trips to the British Library and what he was reading about. About the Commonwealth Immigration Act. About hierarchies of migration from the old dominions and the new commonwealth. About the creation of a National Health Service that depended upon migrant labour. About the preference for white migrant labour. About the reliance on brown migrant labour. About his father being blamed for spreading tuberculosis whilst being paraded as a student learning about tuberculosis. About young men and women lured and looted from one place to another at political whim under the pretence of progress and education. About tabloid headlines of brown doctors killing good British citizens. Honest-working Scots too. About tabloid headlines of Australian doctors and their vouchers. About policies designed to loot brown doctors. About policies designed to discredit brown doctors. About the need to distinguish "good" migrants and "bad" migrants; and how black and brown and white all the migrants were. About how it's impossible not to feel affected, to feel aggrieved. About how he wished he could see his dad again. The Ganjes forever flows, he liked to think.

Viddy placed her hand on Raj's shoulder, as the wind rattled around the waterproof hoods enclosing their bowed heads.

—That's a lot to come to terms with, Raj. And listen, I'm sorry. If before, I didn't, well, listen.

—Don't be sorry. I'm happy now. In a good place. I love Ibti. I just don't know how to feel about being a dad. And it kinda brings all this stuff up in me. But I still feel like something is dead inside. Or, I'm just a bit lost. We're lost. It's hard to imagine a future in London. I dunno if it's my home. Our home. Her home.

—Be easier on yourself. It's the only way through.

In the thick of a sleepless conversation that, in other circumstances, might have veered towards tired glances and uncomfortable embarrassment, Raj and Viddy forgot everything around them for one split second of touch and forgiveness in the unveiled morning light of fragile honesty. They hugged tightly and had almost forgotten about Bobby's predicament, but the embrace did not last long. Peering over Raj's shoulder with tender eyes pointed towards the coast, Viddy startled Raj as she cried out suddenly, dropping her plastic coffee cup as both hands fell motionless, muscles failing her.

—What the fuck! Jesus Christ, thank fuck... For God's sake!

The cup rolled to a halt as the two of them squinted further up the large field to their left, Kilt Rock in the distance. Trundling along the edge, close to the barbed wire fence used to prevent sheep from falling, was Bobby, ivory horn swinging across his chest like a pendulum as he navigated the uneven ground with great purpose. He appeared to be snipping his fingers and gesturing towards a scruffy-looking goat that was circling his legs. Both he and the goat were marching idiosyncratically in the direction of the others. With ceremonial timing, Liam's petite scruffy frame appeared from the opposite direction, as he began to bellow out over the heads of Raj and Viddy, who were trapped in the middle of verbal volleys like a frail and tender tennis net.

—Bobby! Sake, man. Fuck yi doing?! And why huv yi got a goat, fucksake?

—S'nae a goat Liam, ya bam! It's a ram.

—Yi mean a sheep?

—Nae a sheep, a ram.

—Aye, but is a ram no a sheep?

—Are all sheep female?

—Well, aye, suppose. Sheep are lassies and goats are guys, eh?

—Is at some kinda gender neutral stance or are yi just retarded?

—Yi cannae say that anymair, Boaby man.

Bobby looked at Liam with a blend of disdain, shock, and joviality; mouth pulling sideways at the right edge, one eyebrow raised, cheeks dimpled above his beard, both nostrils flaring. He turned to Raj and Viddy, who were now standing behind Liam, still in second state but relieved.

—Youz tellin me you think sheep are the same as goats? What about ewes, then?

The three of them looked puzzled, as if it was a trick question. A pun? A joke? Bobby went on, Doric strains rising.

—How can yinae ken e difference atween a ram, ewe, and goat? Did yi ken the only reason there's mair sheep than people in Scotland is cos the Clearances? Sheep production ower families. But yid need to ken eh difference atween em ti produce.

Raj was smiling. Feeling the Doric rising up within his body and onto his tongue, he indulged Bobby's diatribe.

—Aye, okay, Bobby, wi ken a ewe's a female sheep. Fit aboot mutton, min?

—Yi needin tae eat the ewe the noo, like?

—Nit.

—Well then, there's nae mutton iser, ya fud.

Bobby's adrenaline swirled in a joyful sense of achievement. He had shed the guilt of leaving at the first sight of his friends and was feeling refreshed and quietly accomplished by a sound sleep in the bivvy bag under a cathedral of rock. After an evening walk under the moon, stars, and mist above, Bobby had fallen into a deep slumber, eventually waking to orbs of yellow light that pushed on his eyelids at dawn. He knew there were sheep and goats, maybe even cows and wild Skye dogs around. But it was fine. He knew his mind, and lived with his thoughts, and it was elating to feel so well, so secure. It was even better to see his old friends in the morning, who looked pale and ghostly and lacking sleep. He even managed to navigate Liam's unknowingly insensitive quip about Aberdonians being sheep shaggers. Acknowledging the possible trigger, he quipped back by reminding Liam that the actual statistics of sheep populations in the North-East were, historically at least, far lower than the west of Scotland. So, if fornication with sheep was ever common practice, it was much more likely to occur closer to Glasgow than Aberdeen; a fact reified by the ratio of Glaswegian human males to ewes from the nineteenth century onwards, and so there was no real basis for... Viddy interrupted, calming the nervous conversation down to a more sombre, comforting tone.

—Bobby, you slept? At all?

—Aye. Slept weel!

—Why did you just leave like that? We were worried, man!

—Hud somewhere tae be iday, and frankly couldnae be airsed with all the wee arguments yi were hayin. Like pedantic bairns. S'mair important things to be deein.

—What, like befriending sheep? Or ewes? Or whatever.

—Nihin dishonourable in that, min.

—Why did you stop here?

—Affa bonny, like!

—Really? It was dark when you left.

—S'nae dark noo though, is it! And is it nae affa bonny? Here, we should ging ower to at wee viewpoint and a hae a wee lookie at Kilt Rock, haye, haye.

Bobby's high-pitched inhalation of Doric fairmer "ayes" at the end of the sentence indicated his joviality, feigned or not; and Viddy knew she probably wasn't going to get anywhere by asking him more questions, so she found relief in a burst of laughter.

—Bobby, you're a madman, but aye, let's go take a look at Kilt Rock. It's nice. We may as well since we're here.

Viddy very quickly felt self-conscious about calling Bobby a madman. Sometimes the language comes before the thought forms. He didn't deserve that. But maybe she was just oversensitive or paranoid about her language because of the lack of sleep. Hazy fragility. She watched Bobby from behind, trundling towards the viewpoint, ewe circling around his heels like some shamanic Aberdeenshire Sherpa. He didn't care at all!

He was laughing wildly and, in that moment, it felt good to have old ghosts around again.

The four of them ambled towards the semi-circular viewing platform that overlooked Kilt Rock, arms draped over the rusty iron pipe railings, chins resting down on forearms, fatigued but very much alive. The sun glimmered opaque gold shapes over the Sound of Raasay, across The Minch, and into the Atlantic. A gentle wind gushed through small holes in the railings, emitting a low, haunting drone. It was a beautiful morning. A beautiful sound.

Kilt Rock is made up of large, jagged, overlapping basalt columns, rising up out of a sandstone base resembling, as the signs around them were keen to point out, the plaid patterns of a pleated kilt. Liam thought the colours were cool as fuck; bright red and yellow hues blended together across the rock. Bobby speculated on the name, and Viddy remembered what John would tell her and the twins when they visited. He was so knowledgeable, but always playful with it, a quiet passion for history disguised by a humility. She began to whisper gently over the haunting drone. She began to remember him. His words.

—There's a Gaelic name for this, Creag an Fheilidh. John would always insist we used it. He wanted the twins to know the landscape in Gaelic, said it made you think about it differently, made you closer to it. Closer to something we once knew but might have forgotten.

She looked sombre, chin burrowed in forearms, dark lashes pointing down. Raj, the only one with some grasp of Gaelic, complimented Viddy on her pronunciation, and asked if she got to speak much of it here. Some of her friends were learning; she was too, a bit. It seemed the right thing to do. Or maybe just the popular thing to do. Liam placed one arm across Viddy's shoulders.

—That's cool, Viddy. You must miss him. Cool way to think about land and language, though. You'll always have these memories, his legacy. So will the twins.

The tenderness of Liam's words faded to silence; higher drones wailed from the railings. Viddy smiled.

—Aye, he'd be laughing at us now, for sure. Painting him out to be some Robert Macfarlane character! He'd be cringing.

—He was a cool dude, Viddy. Here's tae him, and to Creag an Fheilidh.

Liam reached into his leather jacket pocket, pulled out a hip flask, poured a drop on the ground before sipping from it and passing it along to Viddy.

—It's about 8 a.m.

—We're on holiday, int we? Fuck it.

They ambled onwards, in ceremonial haze, gazing in the direction of Creag an Fheilidh. Bobby kept quiet through the tenderness, not wanting to disturb it. Never break your tenderness, he reminded himself (was it Jack Keroauc who said that?). All the while he was silently pondering the problems of all this "rewilding" the language of landscape. Just because someone, who usually speaks the Queen's good English, finds a few phrases in an archive, or suddenly begins to fetishise some language or other that might have a few different words for a few different hills; does that really change anything other than their own smug sense of satisfaction? There were no wild places left anyway. Nothing "untouched" by man, including Creag an Fheilidh. Drainage, deforestation, fire, war, famine. An impossibility. And these languages, and the people who actually speak them, aren't "wild" or "closer to nature". Maybe they once were, but Jesus Christ, is everything just cyclical? Have we not been down this road before? Romantic heroes; colonial ethnographers; Jacobites; wild Highlanders; noble savages; primitive tongues; Johnson and Boswell; enraptured white males from Cambridge... remember to get off the merry go round if you feel it moving. Bobby remembered what his therapist had told him. He took a breath and turned to Raj.

—Aye. Creag an Fhukkeeyy...

He laughed at himself for hashing up the pronunciation but persisted.

—Aye, well, does the Gaelic name mean something different?

—Nah. Means Kilt Rock in Gaelic too.

—Aye, okay, but it must've been something before that. Before there were even kilts, I mean. Probably something in Old Norse.

—Aye, maybe. But Creag an Fheilidh suits it. I like that you have some sign of the people and their culture in the landscape. Or have the landscape in the people and culture. It's cool.

—Nae my peoples, onywy!

They all smiled wryly, seemingly in collective remembrance of the graduation ball at Glasgow Uni. They were misfits forced into formality, passing half a bottle of Buckie around, but mainly ripping Bobby for refusing to wear a kilt since "it was nae his peoples", "nae his history" and some "conservative attempt at pan-Scottishness to shore up crown, union, and empire". He did, nonetheless, wear Granda Duthie's clan tartan bow-tie, which Raj was quick to remind him of as he went for a chunder outside before the dances even started. Raj looked at Bobby, unsure if he was responding to his friend in the present, or to some chundering ghost of the past.

—Aye, but it *is* your people, is it not, Bobby? Myth is important. Maybe more important than history. Doesn't matter if they didn't have clan tartans until... whenever – you know the facts better than me. Do you not feel attached to it all?

Bobby thought about the ceilidh again. It was one of the last times they were together, right before Raj left for Berlin. Heed cleared after multiple chunders, Granda Duthie's bow-tie in tact, the night finished with a "Loch Lomond" rammy, arms crossed, kilts flailing, waistcoats creased by the push and pull of bodies as the circle convulsed. He loved that part. Nae his song nor his people, though. Or was it? He thought about James McFadden's goal against France in The Park Bar, saltires waving, Tennent's flailing.

—Aye, spose yi can maybe overthink it all.

Bobby pursed his lips, looking resolute for a moment, before Raj carried on.

—It's weird being away, though. Sometimes wonder if I just cling onto Scotland as a safety anchor, y'know? A fake origin story to pacify myself whenever I feel a bit lost. Sometimes I even put on "Caledonia" whenever I head back down the road, just to feel it. And I kinda hate that. D'yi think everyone feels fraught about where they're from?

Viddy looked towards Raj, eyes wide, thoughtful, nostalgic for something, but she wasn't sure what.

—We're drawn to... no, we absorb and are absorbed by powerful myths. There's a real beauty in it. Stories don't have to be true to mean something special.

—I just don't know what my own story is sometimes, Viddy! My dad was more British than the British. Polite manners, Union Jacks, pictures of the Queen. And aye, they brought the trains to India, y'know!

—Sounds familiar. I guess casteism feeds into that too, though. That striving for status within the establishment...

—Aye, well, I guess I was left to imagine my own roots then. Like, fuck the union, fuck the crown, and fuck the Raj too. Paint me in ash and let me dance wild with the Shaivites! Then after that we can all go to Hampden and sing about fighting and dying for my wee bit hill even though we shat over other people's wee bit hills the world o'er. Probably shat all over the Shaivites hill as well.

—Jesus, Raj.

—Nae Jesus. Shiva for me. Fuck knows, like Bobby says, probably overthinking it.

Raj continued to overthink, or maybe just imagine. He thought about his childhood and playing cricket in Bught Park with his dad, who was never one for football but loved a wicket. A sunny day by the river just west of Culloden – then a few boys with cans cycling by shouting at the "fat bald Paki" who should "just go home". Raj stood rooted to the wickets petrified and watched them head up the bike path towards Culloden. The natives of the north. Proud, heroic, forever brave. Sending them homewards tae think again. Raj felt sad. He was unsure if he was sad in that present moment, looking over to Kilt Rock, or if he was remembering the ghosts that opened his eyes to the cruelties of people, place, and race. He lowered his chin towards his knuckles, rooted himself in the present, and watched the water waltz down and away, and into the Atlantic. The Ganjes forever flows.

Liam, standing to the right of Raj and closest to the cliff face, sprung backwards, sensing a break in conversation.

—Yiz want a charge? Or a wee snack?

Liam offered around his pocket hip flask, reaching into his interior leather pocket again. Bobby refused, citing how much his ivory horn could hold, nae need for refills, plinty Balvenie. Palming down into his side pocket this time, Liam then offered up a few packets of Walker's Shortbread, the type that come free on hotel coffee trays, much to the amusement of Raj whose smile broke the slightly sombre tone that had emerged amidst the morning haze.

—Sake, man! What Travelodge did you rob? Shortbread and all. How appropriate.

—D'yno like shortbread? This tartan shortbread, my friend – and these drones, and our melancholic musings – are as real as we are right now. So fuck yizaw.

—How real's that then, Liam?

—Well, that's all subjective, innit.

Liam pushed himself back and forth on the railing, feeling his hands get colder whilst looking at his watch.

—Fuckin hell, man. We've been staring at this rock for about an hour! We'll no get that hour back today, or ever.

Bobby shook his head.

—I hate that phrase. Phit oors have yi ever gotten back? At's jist time. Oors go by and we don't see them again. Iver. Phit why do people insist on at?

—Aye, right enough, Boaby, ma man.

—But onyways, I've got somewhere tae be, so aye, let's get going.

With collective ceremony, they unwrapped their pocket-size shortbread, product of Scotland, established in 1898, and washed down the sugary fragments with a wee morning nip.

WHO BY FIRE

The breath of heavenly
bodies is not only in the wind
but in fire and flame and folklore.
Hands, feet, stars, meteorites, moons,
and mindsets can fade in the darkening
of shadow-grass; be seen in the flames of
a passing night; burn in the embers of a tinder-
branch; and blaze above a reed-torch that shines
light on the hiding places of old ghosts. Yet fire, too,
is more than a utility. More than microseconds, minutes,
hours, days, and years. It burns and ashes and burns
and ashes again until dark becomes light in the
passing of a night. After about five or maybe
forty-five minutes of morning conversation,
the Kirtankara set off for Staffin, like a
cobra coiling up the isle in
search of its final meal.

Bobby convinced the others to stop off just outside of Staffin at a cottage that had been converted into a wellness retreat. He'd read about it and wanted to see if it might be somewhere he would return to whenever he got a hankering for wellbeing consumerism, which occasionally occurred during his brown bean cushion reveries. Viddy was quietly sceptical, having grown tired of the island's yoga retreats, "wild" escapes, and expensive week-long lessons on how to plant crops according to the phases of the moon. But she also knew they gave new life to the community, to tourism, and that the intentions were pure. Besides, she was happy for Bobby, glad he was thinking about wellbeing, wellness, and his future. Riding Nicholson, eyes to sky, Bobby held onto the back of her bike as she clunked through the gears, following Liam's lead further up the A855.

Raj, cautious and tired, with the taste of whisky and shortbread on his tongue, tailed behind slowly, mostly enjoying the ride. Far from the relaxing reunion they had talked about, he was at least feeling alive again, present in a way that had evaded him of late. Dull clouds formed above, and a quiet sadness crept back in. Perhaps he was just missing Ibti, plump in belly. They were in love, loyal to each other, and it was a wondrous thing to welcome another soul into the world. To be part of that. It was the first time he'd thought of them properly, untainted by his own hang-ups, since arriving. He missed the warmth and banality of cycling home from work, painting the spare room and arguing about what to watch on television, and whether or not it would have Portuguese subtitles. She had joked about Viddy before he left. Told him not to fall back into old ways. Ibti was cool, though. She understood. It had been hard to be anything but a little distant with Viddy fat first, but he felt better after their chat at Kilt Rock. He rattled into fourth and popped the clutch a little too early, producing a harsh bursting sound as he traced the wisps of Viddy's hair up ahead, and the large curve of Bobby's back which obscured the rest of her. That's just the nature of those old ghosts. The most intense ones, the ones who lit us inside and kissed us outside. They haunt us the most, threaten our future through the possibilities of another past or, at worst, another future. He thought again of Ibti's plump belly and felt sad and glad and confused and alive.

Leading the way, Liam was easy on the revs and anxious on the turns. He'd had enough petty spats in the past not to want any bad brushes with island polis, and he could still smell the morning nip in his own helmet, which seemed to be mingling with exhaust fumes to create a heady cocktail of smog. It would be good to get off the road soon. He glimpsed a fleeting black shape in his right rear-view mirror and was startled, imagining a beastly raven intent on pecking the eyes out of a lamb. He'd heard stories about vicious ravens on Skye but was never quite sure if they were mythical or not. The islands were like that to him. As much as he tried not to romanticise or mystify them, he remained mystical and romantic. Perhaps it was a wilful ignorance. Wilful imagining. The black outline cast quickly back and forth across the mirror again, but this time it was on the left-hand side. Thankfully, it wasn't a raven, but Bobby. He was signalling from the back of Viddy's bike to take the next right. His exaggerated movements resembled a drunken YMCA dancer, ivory horn flailing in the wind, left arm forming a black arc across the mirror. They must have been close. It would be good to get off the road. He hoped this wellness place had a café with strong espresso.

They parked their bikes in a line on the loose gravel car park of the Skye Mind Healers' Retreat. The building was dirty-white and isolated, if not majestic, amidst barren fields and stone dykes overlooking Staffin Bay. It was clearly a popular spot judging by the electric bikes, BMWs, and Teslas recharging outside. Liam asked Bobby if it might be too busy to bother going in. It didn't look like they had a café and, if anything, there seemed to be a private function or event this weekend, but Bobby was adamant.

—Nah nah, min. At's why we're here. Time is it? Quarter past eliven? Tidy, kicks aff at twelve, ahink. Time for a quick bine and...

—Whit?

Bobby stood rolling calmly as Liam fired a round of questions about what was going on and if he was alright. They could call someone if he needed help. Bobby calmly finished scrunching down his rollie, licking the sticky edge with delicacy, and thumbing the fold down with precision before he responded. Composed and holding court.

—It's sound. Booked us into a wellness retreat for the afternoon. Four o us. Paid for it with ma last paycheck, as weel. S'why I've been so skint this month!

—A fuckin wellness retreat? Fucksake, Bobby, are we not well enough just riding around a bit?

—It'll be sound.

—Fuck me, man. How long you had this planned? And could yi no have said? Am into retreats but need to know a wee bit in advance. Av had two drams this morning, fucksake!

—Booked it a couple weeks ago. Thought we could ah do with a break. Feel the chi, realign oor chakras.

Bobby closed his eyes. He exhaled deeply and drew his left hand towards his chest, just below the ivory horn, rollie now tucked into his right palm. It was unclear to the others whether to laugh or throw some tenderness towards a thoughtful gesture all bound up in the stoic features of Bobby's beardy face.

Raj was quiet, high cheekbones protruding through a restrained lippy smile. Viddy was curious, if a little put off by the fact that she probably knew some of the others inside. Surely some of the SCWSC would be there, but then again Freya hadn't mentioned it. It was exactly the type of thing she regularly told Viddy to do. And exactly the type of thing Viddy would find a way to avoid. Thank God the twins' rabidity was good for something. Then again, her very avoidance of Freya and the others was starting to feel hollow, particularly in the wake of a whimsical motorcycle ride where she'd dumped the twins on her and left without much of a whisper. She felt guilty. For Freya. For John. For failing to see beyond herself. Viddy thought of the Halloween party Freya held at her house for them and another couple, Meg and Rich, three years ago, before the twins.

Meg had grown up in Skye but moved to London to study fine art, where she met Rich, a musician living in a Camberwell squat. Contrary to her hopes and dreams of escaping life on the island, Rich convinced Meg to go back and begin crofting, in the hope of opening an organic food co-op. There were subsidies for it. It would be hard, but meaningful. He'd always wanted away from the city. They adapted and grafted, working the land, wool, sold cakes on Sundays, and Rich even took the occasional shift at the coffee shop in Portree to make ends meet. All for the greater good. Their own little independent store front. After three years, they almost had enough for a deposit. Meg and Rich met Freya at a yoga class in the town hall soon after moving up.

Freya had grown up in Cambridgeshire and had no links to Skye before moving, but she was intent on developing a permaculture smallholding there after finishing a degree in earth sciences. Freya was smart, driven, enthusiastic, and outwardly sensitive while inwardly resolute. She was well aware of the utopian honeymooners who moved to "remote parts" of the Highlands and Islands only to scuttle back to England with a hot water bottle between their legs come the first winter. She thought she was different. And she was. Three years in, Freya had started more community groups than Christ could swing a cat at. She worked hard to form relationships, united different people, attended town hall meetings, and opposed commercial plans from big companies intent on building houses for rent. Any community worth its own integrity would benefit from Freya.

Viddy enjoyed hanging out with Freya, Meg, and Rich in the early days on Skye. There was an infectious energy around their work ethic, ideals, and willingness to walk beyond their comfort zones. But she always felt more comfortable when she was alone with them. Or rather, when

John wasn't around. She felt guilt at this realisation, now that he was gone. What a treacherous person she had been. These small acts. So pitiful. So self-absorbed. And she blamed herself. It was nothing to do with John at all. He actually liked meeting up with the others. It was Viddy that had woven some narrative of awkwardness around their meet-ups. Maybe she just wanted some space. How awful.

The night of Freya's Halloween party was one of the last times John hung out with them all, partly because he knew Viddy didn't seem herself when he was around. They had walked into Freya's house to the sound of Joy Division's "Dead Souls" blaring from the kitchen. It was one of the songs Rich had put on his Halloween playlist. John and Viddy walked into the kitchen wielding red wine and pumpkin pie dessert to find Rich and Freya in a friendly but increasingly heated debate about whether or not the song was recorded the night before Ian Curtis committed suicide. Meanwhile, Meg, petite and pixie-like with spiky blonde hair and glittery eyeshadow, danced around by herself, allowing her rhythmical neck movements to lead her around different parts of the room, flailing her arms above her head in a disjointed but alluring fashion. Shouting over the music, Rich drew John and Viddy into the conversation.

—So, what do you guys think? Surely it's a mythology! Can't have been recorded then.

Viddy jumped in awkwardly, replying in a more panicked tone than she realised.

—Och, who knows! I doubt John even knows who Ian Curtis is! Do you?

—Eh, aye... but am no sure about that. Sorry.

The moment passed but it was one of a series that

night in which Viddy would presuppose what John would or wouldn't know; how he could or couldn't connect to people in the way she could. They didn't spend much of the evening together after that. John got into an enthusiastic and genuinely warm conversation with Rich about his love for The KLF; while Viddy let Meg paint her face with glitter and turned the music up to spare hearing anything she might find embarrassing. Embarrassing. How could she have ever found him embarrassing? In hindsight, she hated herself for that. And perhaps it was the hate that was doing it now. A hate towards herself, rather than others, that led her to shun those who wanted to nurture her most in a time of deep grief.

Viddy, conscious she was lost in her own thoughts, palmed at the side of her cheek and turned her attention back to Bobby's wellness retreat.

—So, is it, like, yoga? Or meditation?

—Think it's ahin.

—Was it expensive?

—300£ a pop.

—Bobby, 300£ each?

—Aye.

—Bobby! That's 200,1£!

—At's maths! At's also aboot my monthly wage. Which is why I could only buy a few rowies for the road.

—And it's for one afternoon? Bobby, it's just too much. I mean, surely, we can just...

—Just gee it time. Time is phit we should gie it, haye, haye.

Bobby's high-pitched inhalations of Doric fairmer "ayes" at the end of the sentence settled it. He'd invested. It was thoughtful, and he wanted, Viddy thought, gratitude rather than moans about the expense. Just like the gaunt man carrying their suitcase. This was Bobby at his most thoughtful. And most ridiculous. Viddy shook out her thick black hair from the tassled scarf that was restraining it from flapping over forehead and turned to the others.

—Mon then, team. Let's get well.

Bobby led the way, chapping on the green wooden door to no response, before gently creeping into a square foyer that had been converted into a reception. He was, often unexpectedly, light as a ballerina on his toes when he wanted to be, and his entrance indicated a manner of respect and delicacy. An upcycled desk, made from splintered pallets, stood in the middle of the foyer and was scattered with a selection of leaflets detailing times, dates, tables, and bullet-point benefits for the open-hearted travellers trapsing through the doors.

THE SKYE MIND HEALERS' RETREAT

- Introduction to Plant Medicine
- Realigning with your Higher Self
- Meeting your Inner Child
- Past Life Regression
- Future Life Progression
- Soul Retrieval
- Energy Extraction
- Unveiling the Shadow
- Spirit Releasement
- Breaking Soul Ties
- Parallel Realities

- Intuitive Solutions
- Visionary Art Explorations
- Yoga sessions
- Guided meditations/visualisations
- Group Sharing

Liam was first to comment as the others leafed through, trying to comprehend how concepts like "Spirit Releasement" could be reduced to a bullet-point, or even to language.

—We gonnae get high here, Boaby? Seems far out.

Before Bobby could reply, a tall, bony figure appeared. Long hair, bearded, big cheekbones, glowing smile, beads, and a whispy-haired chest. He had entered the corridor from a side door they hadn't seen. He spoke softly, too softly, in some strange American accent, possibly Californian but hard to place. Short, abrupt sentences. Too abrupt. Too profound.

—Hello. My dear friends. Here to join for the afternoon ceremony. Please. Welcome. Relax. There is tea in the kitchen. Do not eat anymore. Let us cleanse.

Bobby sensed hesitance, concern, and repressed laughter among the others, but nevertheless followed the bony man through the back, past a groaning room, and into a quiet kitchen area where plastic orange chairs were arranged in an imperfect circle.

Between the corridor and kitchen, Viddy pondered why there always had to be a skinny bearded man in places like these. The second one on this trip as well! Some kind of Jesus complex, perhaps. How did one man's essence, myth, being, and goddamn look – skinny, bearded, linen, beads, eyes that don't blink – become so ideologically persistent in emanating the spiritual divine? It was just short of nauseating to her. Now, at least, if not always. She thought of how attracted she was to Raj around ten years ago. The flowing dark locks, olive skin, Shiva pendant, and misty-eyed discussions about Buddha at midnight. Maybe it was youthful naïvety. Or maybe reading *Zealot* later in life made her think that art and image in thy name were all just part of some patriarchal ploy. Art depicting chaos situations. Loyal followings. Total regard for a suffering male leader who offers a path to salvation. But anyway, let's have a cup of tea in the kitchen.

They sat quietly and nervously in the yellow-tiled kitchen, each taking turns to pour from the herbal teapot into little handless clay cups. Bony man was now sitting behind the circle in apparent omniscience. He introduced himself as Ethan, and began to speak between sips, asking them questions about diet, red meat, alcohol consumption, depression, and health histories that none of the four answered honestly. Not least because of the morning drams and bacon baps (which are cultural and ca be replaced). A clipboard was passed around.

—Let us begin with some yoga. Before the transition.

Ethan sprang from the table he was sitting on, revealing aggressively tanned calf muscles and an ankle tattoo of a gecko. He led the others back in the direction of flailing groans, retching, tears, sobbing, and some kind of chanting. As if commanded by the sense of ceremony, they all followed him silently and without protest, in procession, through the corridor, catching a glimpse of a dimly lit room with its door ajar. Mattresses lined the walls. Two people were passed out.

Another squirmed around in the fetal position, and two burly men were gripping each other's bald heads, sobbing loudly, salivating over each other's white robes. Bobby scuttled past quickly, as did Raj and Viddy, unsure, in the moment, if it was rude to stop. Liam, treading more slowly behind, stopped for a few seconds longer outside the door. He listened as someone droned a throaty melody in some unfamiliar language. They were also, by the sounds of it, shaking maracas, pounding mortar, and foot-stomping at the same time. Liam shuffled onwards to join the others in the adjacent room. The crunching rhythm of mortar-maracas and stench of vomit receded as he shut the door to find them stood over five yoga mats. Ethan was at the helm, perched in front of a window, sunbeams breaking through the grey clouds.

—I want to begin.

They were all nervous, but only Liam spoke.

—Don't let us stop yi, ma man. Begin away. We'll begin with yi and...

—Okay. Quiet. As you stretch. Into downward dog. Ask. *What do I want to learn about myself?*

They followed Ethan's lead, exhaling and stretching down onto their palms. Bobby's arse was high in the air above Liam's head, horn by his side. They hadn't realised Ethan wanted them to repeat the question out loud, but after gentle encouragement they did so in unison.

What do I want to learn about myself?

Viddy, head between her arms, looking backwards through her legs, smiled at Raj as Ethan continued to speak gently, slowly. Too gently, too slowly.

—Now. As you come back. Into Child's Pose. Ask. *Show me who I've become.* They each repeated after him four times.

> *Show me who I've become.*
> *Show me who I've become.*
> *Show me who I've become.*
> *Show me who I've become.*

Then deep inhales. Exhales. Pursed smiles all round. Viddy, increasingly creeped out by Ethan, was hoping the request to "show me" was directed towards her inner self rather than the poundshop Jesus in front of her; while Bobby, more serious between his breaths (he'd paid for this shit) began to think about the emancipatory possibilities of having someone guide him along a path. Maybe Ethan could help unveil the shadow, as the leaflet said. Though he was unsure what that even meant, or what the shadow was.

Liam's skinny frame curved back to Child's Pose as Raj and Viddy sat up, looking weary. Liam, particularly after kicking his habits, had become fairly proficient in Hatha yoga and meditation. The unlikely Yogi fae the Drum, he liked to think, while consciously aware of countless others. He'd even started a Vipassanā instructor course and embraced the inevitable introspection of prolonged silence. It was a good way to travel and make a living. Lord knows how the rich loved to splurge on a two-week silent retreat in Costa Rica. He'd be there at the helm, helping prepare their meals. He might even find himself in a position like Ethan's soon. So why did things feel so off? Maybe it was the morning dram. Instead of realigning the chakras it made them dance around his body. But that was cool too, was it not? He inhaled deeply, rising out of Child's Pose, exhaling into an upright elegant posture, and cupping his praying hands to his nose. *Namaste*. Ethan smiled and ushered them through to a room next to the retching maraca-mortar affair.

The room they entered was lined with crimson drapes, lit with large candles, and featured a straw altar which Ethan perched behind, cross-legged. An imperfectly circular large wooden bowl was placed on the altar, beside smaller bowls of woodchippings, vines, shrubs, leaves, and a steel ladle which reminded Bobby of the serving instruments used to slop out cal mashed tatties and kilted sausages in high school. Slumped up against the four draping walls were four groggy mattresses, each with a toilet roll, paisley-pattern robe, and oddly shaped red plastic containers next to them, resembling mop-buckets with the mops removed. They sat on the four yoga mats lined across the room and quietly observed Ethan as he rose slowly from his cross-legged position with ceremonial poise and turned around to reach between the drapes behind him. He unfolded a robe embroidered with intricate, fluorescent geometric patterns and slipped it around his shoulders. At this point, Liam noticed just how aggressively fluorescent Ethan's face and teeth were, as he began to verbally flaunt his qualifications in ceremonial plant medicine from an unspecified indigenous tribe in an unspecified region of the remote Peruvian rainforest.

Against the squeals, retches, sobs, and mortar-maracas of the adjacent room, Ethan gently stirred his brew around with the dinner-lady ladle, whilst describing the process of purification which was to come. It would encompass equal parts joy and suffering. Sometimes the shame and pain of others would come upon the self. Sometimes the self would liberate itself from the pain and shame of others. A song might sound exquisitely beautiful, but also so painful to the point of purging it from ear and body. (Bobby, one eyebrow raised, wondered if anyone had actually chundered oot a lug.) This would be the most honest mirror ever seen. For a true mirror is not static in reflection, but bends inwards and outwards, backwards and forwards. (Bobby thought of Codona's Funhouse.) More fluorescent teeth.

—Please. Take a robe. Begin to ask. Again. *Show me who I've become.*

With collective unease, they quietly wrapped the robes around themselves, nervous energy pulsing through the room and the bodies within it. More teeth, more stirring. More teeth.

—Selfhood is an illusion. There is no fixed self, no thinker behind our thoughts. Selfhood is illusion. And to face the illusion is to find new presence. New peace. Dissolve the body. The bearer of mental states. Beyond.

More retches from the other room, more fluorescent teeth.

—And so let us be together. And apart. And begin.

Ethan scooped into the wooden bowl with his dinner-lady ladle, carefully transferring a sticky brown liquid into an old plastic cola bottle, before blowing across its top, causing a wispy whistle to reverberate around the room. He took a small sip. With his left hand, he gestured for someone to come forward to continue the ceremony. Raj bowed his head like a schoolchild trying to avoid the attention of a teacher. Bobby, sitting furthest left, looked pensive, twirling the ends of his unkempt beard. In between, Liam and Viddy waited, glancing sideways at each other for any indication of other bodies that might rise before them. None did and, with fumbling synchronicity, their legs stumbled into each other as they rocked forward and up from their yoga mats at the same time. Nervous laughter. Congenial caution.

—Sorry, Viddy, pal, on yi go.

—No, honestly, you first, seems better. Go for it, Liam. Godspeed, or whatever!

Liam exhaled, puffed out his cheeks, raked his hair, then mindfully watched his feet as they crept one after the other, bringing him closer to Ethan, who, with great ceremony, lifted the dinner-lady ladle above his head. His robe draped below both elbows like geometric wings. Yelping some throaty chant, he proceeded to pour a small mouthful of the thick brown liquid into Liam's mouth, who was now kneeling before him like a helpless baby bird. The brown liquid flowed slowly onto his tongue, and he immediately thought of the Royal Enfield Liquid Gun Oil James had given him yesterday. Yesterday, Jesus. Was that just yesterday he was in James's garage in Drumry? The sour, twiggy taste of the thick liquid rooted him to the present. The texture was oily and earthy and hard to swallow, like a tea brewed with muddy rainwater and damp forest foliage. He struggled to swallow and welcomed the small cup of water which Ethan handed him with a simultaneous gesture towards the mattress, which Liam embraced slowly, sliding his back down the wall, resting back in expectation.

Ethan gestured towards Bobby. It was his turn to sample the psychedelic soup. Ethan lay the dinner-lady ladle down and held both palms out towards Bobby, all the while continuing his deep throaty chant in anticipation of a cross-legged rise. But Bobby looked despondent, head shaking from side to side, lips curled, small fat nostrils flaring.

—Nah. Ca dee it.

Liam, unfazed by his first few sips but fazed immensely by Bobby's response, jolted forward from the mattress.

—Whitdya mean yi cannae dee it? Av just downed a cup o earthwater cuz you paid fur it!

—Nah. Jist ca. Jist ca dee it.

—How?!

—Jist ca.

—So am sposed tae sit and whitey in the corner here masel? Fucksake, man.

Viddy glanced at Liam, then back to Bobby, ignoring Ethan who was continuing to chant his wavering throaty chant, which was sounding increasingly broken and higher pitched. More retches from the other room. Viddy spoke over them.

—Why you not up for it, Bobby? We're here now, so might as well?

—Nae sure. Are we? Here?

—How'd you mean?

—Well, that's the whole point is it nae? Finding oot there's no unified self, just a series of transient feelings, memories, and impressions of the past and future? I'm just nae sure I need to chunder into a void of darkness to feel better about that. Davy Hume said it afore and I'm sayin it noo... nae need for a massive chunder.

—It could be cool? And you've paid for it!

Liam flung his head back in disbelief at the debate before

him, ruffled, puffing upwards, hot, anxious, perspiring. Ethan's chant rose to an even higher and more wavering pitch, while Bobby continued to reason with careful eloquence.

—It jist seems an extreme way of acknowledging the absence of an abiding sel. Aye, it may take *dukkha* – at's suffering, by the way – to realise that bodies, minds, mates, and selves come and go, but I've suffered enough. Am jist needin a bine noo, to be honest.

—But I suppose there are several ways to reach that type of non-selfhood? It just seems if we are here, we may as well...

Raj, who had remained quiet, pushed himself back against the wall opposite Liam, who was continuing to perspire profusely. He chimed in.

—It's just a bit weird. Cherry-picking indigenous customs and pretending that they'll profoundly change the way we look at the world, or ourselves, or whatever. Seems like an expensive way to get high. And I bet a lot of folks are making money off it too.

Ethan's chant rose to a crescendo as his eyes opened with stern severity. The throaty inner peace had dissipated, and he spoke in quicker, fluid, more coherent sentences. Aggressive fluorescent teeth.

—Did you know that consuming ayahuasca once weekly for a month is as effective as an eight-week mindfulness program? And that it is scientifically proven to reduce depression and anxiety?

Bobby, jarred by Ethan's robotic tone, rose to his feet.

—Aye, fair enough. Jist nae needin to spew ma ringer to feel better about masel today, ken. Sorry, nae up for it. Can I just get a bit o money back? Tak phit yi need fir Liam's shot.

A chaotic energy fizzed around the room as Ethan, reaching again beyond the red velvet drapes, flicked a light switch, which startled the continually perspiring Liam, now covering his eyes with his forearms, hiding from the light, embracing the dark. Viddy, initially the most spooked by Ethan, took on a downbeat, sensitive tone as they began to disrobe and gather their belongings and make peace.

—Look, we don't want to disrespect you, or the sacred ceremony, in anyway. We've had a bit of a long night. It's just not the right time.

—Well, if you want to go on choosing ignorance, go ahead.

—Excuse me?

—Refusing to acknowledge your inner self, your past, what made you, what makes you. It's ignorance.

—It's also ignorant to be tone deaf to the present moment.

—Meaning?

—Meaning you're a sham artist for trying to force people into something!

—You little bitch!

—What the fuck?! What the fuck did you call me?!

—Just get out, please.

Ethan frantically rolled up the yoga mats in a rage, shooing the others out of the room whilst Viddy stood and glared and flared like Parvati in full fire and flame and ready to rip his head off.

—You have no fucking idea. No fucking idea at all!

Viddy refused to grant Ethan her holy river of tears, holding back before turning about swiftly and bursting out the front door; raging, crying, and raging some more.

Inside, Bobby remained cross-legged, rocking against the wall, nervous, concerned, and feeling guilty for causing the whole fiasco. Raj, meanwhile, struggled to repress his anger to the point of feeling drained, weak, and ready to leave. He just wanted to settle up and get out of there. Get them all out of there.

—Look, Ethan. You've insulted one friend and apparently poisoned another. We'll not take up any more of your time. Let's just settle up so we can go now, eh?

After a quietly aggressive retort about how they would never understand the true meaning of time at all, Ethan, all fluorescent teeth, beads, bones, beard, and straggly hair, feigned a patronising smile as he reassured them that their comfort came first, and perhaps they could return again when the universe allowed. With a swift smartphone card transaction, the ceremony came to a close. Raj and Viddy took an arm each of Liam, who was now stumbling, mumbling, and giggling his way back to the front door of the the Skye Mind Healers' Retreat.

It would be good to get some fresh air.

They needed to breathe.

TAKE THIS LONGING

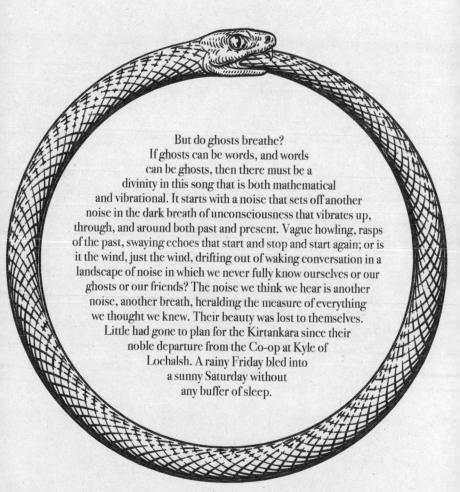

But do ghosts breathe?
If ghosts can be words, and words
can be ghosts, then there must be a
divinity in this song that is both mathematical
and vibrational. It starts with a noise that sets off another
noise in the dark breath of unconsciousness that vibrates up,
through, and around both past and present. Vague howling, rasps
of the past, swaying echoes that start and stop and start again; or is
it the wind, just the wind, drifting out of waking conversation in a
landscape of noise in which we never fully know ourselves or our
ghosts or our friends? The noise we think we hear is another
noise, another breath, heralding the measure of everything
we thought we knew. Their beauty was lost to themselves.
Little had gone to plan for the Kirtankara since their
noble departure from the Co-op at Kyle of
Lochalsh. A rainy Friday bled into
a sunny Saturday without
any buffer of sleep.

◯

Liam perched on a large erratic rock at the edge of the Skye
Mind Healers' Retreat car park, a few yards away from the
Royal Enfield Bullets. They looked lost, tired, and beautiful
in the afternoon sun, which winked and reflected across
chrome tanks, silver handlebars, and draped helmets. The
others stood around Liam in expectation, or maybe fas-
cination, for what might come, but it was mainly nausea,
sweat, tiredness, and damp heroics.

—I'll be sound. Honestly, am awrite.

Viddy's eyes were puffy and sad as she gazed back at
Liam, now shivering more feverishly and helplessly than
before. It reminded her of a deer she and John had hit and
injured once. The sadness of the shake, the morbidity of
the shiver, as they waited for it to die on a black island night
lit up by damaged Defender headlamps.

—Liam, are you okay? It's just, I can't, we can't, I can't...

Viddy coiled her head inwards to her chest, then grasped
at her hair with two hands and began quivering, quietly weeping. A flood of death and deaths and despair and pain seemed
to ripple through her in that moment. She sobbed, fell to her
knees, and sobbed some more. Bobby knelt beside her. He
sobbed too, and spoke gently, placing a hand on her shoulder.

—Am sorry, quine. It's ma fault. Ah that pish in there. Ay
fuckin up, it seems, eh.

Viddy pressed her head against Bobby's shoulder, tears
turning to a momentarily giggle and consoling sniffle.

—It's not that, Bobby. It's just everything. I've been trying not to cry. Trying not to remember. How fucked up is that?

—Nae fucked up, Viddy. It's hard to cry when you have to be strong. You keep your skin thick fir the sake o itthers. Fir the sake o the twins. It's beautiful, ken.

—Ach, Bobby. Sometimes I just wish I could just rip all the skin away. Feel raw and sore. Feel something again. It's hard.

—I hear yi, quine. Took ages for me to get a handle on keepin masel sane. Ken av been in and oot of therapy fir years now?

—Yeh, I guess I did. Feel guilty for not asking much about it.

—Ach, nothing to ask. Wiz a slave to ma thoughts. At's it. I'm a wee bit mair free now. But yi niver ken, eh.

—You seem well, Bobby. It gives me hope, somehow. Here, though. Seriously, is Liam going to be alright?

Amidst their intimate reflections, Liam had bolted behind the house. Bobby stood up, lit a rollie, and began nervously sucking on it while wondering if they should go check on him. Raj crunched quietly over the gravel to stand next to Bobby, who was now joined by an upright and little more spritely Viddy. The three of them gazed in the direction of the house. They couldn't see Liam but continued to stare anyway, dazed and hazed, with Raj muttering his way into the conversation.

—I get yi, Viddy.

—Get what?

—I get how hard it is not to feel. It's been weird for me lately.

—Yeh. Guess there's a lot to process.

—There's not really. Maybe for you there is. I'm just an eejit.

—An eejit?

—Aye.

—Okay. Here, though. Really, is he gonna be okay? Liam, I mean. Listen!

—Reckon he'll be sound. He's just chundering.

The cold wind blew against their cheeks as they listened to retches and coughy

gurns. The wind stung nicely; the sun was crisp. They were tired and sleepless and helpless, but a fragile feeling of safety began to inexplicably emerge between them even as Liam was emptying his body. The bright Skye blues and greens began to streak with a few hints of crimson. It was 4 p.m. already. Had they really been inside for that long? It was hard to tell when they had barely slept. No respite to distort or disrupt the bodily sensation of being alive. Raj was feeling surprisingly bright, but the same couldn't be said for Liam who was traipsing back, dishevelled, perspiring, and attempting to fasten the unbuckled brown belt wound around his skinny black jeans.

—Got the shits anaw, man.

—Shit, man. Did yi take a shit on the house?!

—No sure. Bad though. Smelt like a dead animal.

—How yi feeling?

—Shite, man. Feels like my face is oan fire.

—Feeling spiritual? Any different?

—Aye, about two stone lighter, mate.

Liam gingerly perched down on the erratic rock opposite the Enfields, which were now glowing shades of orange amidst silver and yellow and white dusk sparkles. The air was colder, and the idea of asking Ethan for a few spare beds for the night was raised. Get some rest, recoup, regroup. Viddy shot the idea down immediately with trident fire and flame, prompting smiles from the others. The wrath of Parvati.

—No way am going to see that fuckin wee Jesus creep again. Fuckin fraud. You know what sucks most? Is that I actually really want to do ayahuasca. I think it could be truly sacred, you know?

Raj smiled at her. Her fire. Her flame. Her glowing.

—I dunno. I dunno too much about it. Maybe I was unfair before. The truth is I'm probably just scared to see into myself so deeply at the moment. If that's what it does.

—I just feel ready to exorcise myself of things I repress. Things that occupy me but escape my consciousness. Facing up to things again instead of burying them. A cleanse.

—You think it could be like that?

—I think seeing yourself from another perspective could be truly sacred, sure.

—Ethan wasn't so sacred, was he?

—That's what's so fuckin annoying! Creepy sham artist. I have these friends. I met them on a farm in France a few years ago. Anyway, they do it every year at a retreat in the mountains of Brazil. No electricity. Cabins. Wild dogs. Dancing. Serenity. They say it's beautiful. Like a reset. Like being born into a new self every year.

—Sounds intense. Think I have all the new births I need for now.

—Yeh. That's fair enough. Luckily our man Ethan wasn't up to the ceremony.

Bobby mumbled an apology for the failed health retreat fiasco amidst an emergent collegiality that was growing stronger among them. Nothing much had gone to plan, but that was okay. The plan, as Liam's open-mapped gesticulations at Kyle of Lochalsh had it at least, was to have looped around the north-east coast of the island by Saturday night, taking in a leisurely ride along the wee road up past Duntulm, Kilmuir, and winding down to Uig by dark, where they could have a few pints, a pub meal, and restore themselves for the journey back down the A87 the next day.

—At's nae happening.

Bobby thumbed and pinched at the map on his phone, last remnants of the tight rollie sooked up to his lips. Raj had a train back to London on Sunday night from Glasgow, and Viddy had to collect the twins from Freya. They would have to about turn back down the road. Liam started to mumble, in some strangely profound tone.

—*And sorry I could not travel both...*

—Fit?

—*And looked down one...*

—Aye, okay.

Bobby smiled at Raj and Viddy. He felt both sympathy and envy for Liam, head down in sweaty reverie, a little transcendental. Nevertheless, Bobby had a new burst of energy and kept pinching at his maps to determine where they might go, if anywhere at all.

—Didyae ken that it's only about an hour or so from here back to Kyle of Lochalsh?

Viddy knew all too well, but it sounded no less surprising to her than to Raj. They had left on Friday morning, and it was now Saturday. But they had only travelled for about an hour on the bikes. In this sleepless state it was hard to comprehend what happened in between, as time stretched and convulsed and accelerated. It was almost time to go home, to leave each other again. A sense of collective depletion coursed through them, perhaps a sadness at the failure to move forward quickly enough, with the opportunity to do so dissipating, dissolving. They would soon be ghosts again. Turning her head towards a pinking sky, Viddy felt a burst of sadness, but one she wanted to harness. Nah. They wouldn't stay here with that freak Ethan.

She knew where they could go.

She just wasn't sure if she could manage.

As the months passed by like dark shadows in the wake of John's death, Viddy wanted him to die more each day. Die properly. Die into nothing, die into the dead and black forever. Saving him was just too hard. The paradoxical and impossible pressure to keep his light around her and the twins became too much. It was a huge burden to keep him alive, and it became a stone in her heart, weighing down heavier with each tired day and waking night. It seemed to be all on her. His life was at her mercy; she could choose to remember his name or recount his being at whatever whim seemed possible at any given moment. It was all too much.

It was partly why things had gotten so hard with Freya and her friends at the SCWSC. Freya had never mentioned John again after the slightly awkward candlelit vigil in Staffin, where Viddy said little, smiled less, and left without a tear. It seemed like Viddy didn't want to talk, and so swims and cakes and knits became the objects of empathy that displaced any meaningful conversation. But it wasn't necessarily the case that Viddy didn't want to talk. It was the expectation that she should that paralysed her. The guilt that her memories were the only help left to him; she alone was the only one capable of recoiling the snaking ropes that plunged him into the icy cold depths which plundered his lungs, body, and breath into submission. He constantly needed saving, from the ropes, from the twins, from Freya, and his family. And she wanted him to die. So, she banished the records they once danced to, the biscuits they watched films with, and avoided the nooks and crannies of land where the memories that haunted her were made. There were, though, glimmers of reprieve from this paralytic predicament.

Viddy was paying occasional visits to Alec and Mairi's croft just outside Fiscavaig. They were an older couple. Alec was originally from Skye "or at least as far back as the family tree goes", and Mairi from Harris, but a Skye resident for over twenty years. Alec was onboard, the day of John's accident. His face had since swelled downwards into a solemnity that matched the stoicism of his stout frame, sparse language, and black rubber boots. They had gotten to know John and Viddy just after the birth of the twins, partly because they also had two twin boys who were now off thriving on scholarships at some American university. Amidst the pointed advice about changing two nappies at once, Viddy had initially seen an older version of herself and John in them. Fishing, crofting, knitting. Taking summer trips to see what their wild boys were up to in another part of the world. Wondering if they might ever return. But all that was a dream deferred. No, a dead dream. A dream she needed to be dead.

Most days when Viddy visited the croft at Fiscavaig, Alec would say a solemn hello-and-how-you-keeping before trotting out to the barn. There was always work to be done. Work had always helped. It meant that Viddy wound up spending a lot of time with Mairi. Sparse but meaningful exchanges amidst the soporific sounds of spinning wool, knitting needles, graphite, ink, and paint. Mairi divided her time between helping with the croft and carving out two successful careers as the manager of a successful yarn company and abstract painter. Her versatility, hardy resolve, and fragments of a wild and well-travelled past immediately drew a form of affection from Viddy that fired her own aspirations. Over cups of tea Mairi would occasionally let slip some anecdote about running away to India when she was nineteen back in her "wilder days", but never with an ounce of worldly self-aggrandisement. Viddy would sit quietly, smiling and observing Mairi's face as she worked at something or other on the oak kitchen table. Two bulbous cheekbones offset by beautifully greying blonde hair. Deep-blue fairy pool eyes. Gently wrinkled hands at once elegant and well worked. Viddy imagined her as being imbibed with the power, beauty, and capability of Hebridean witches long past. Strong and beautiful women ideologically rebuked on the basis of their charismatic strength and capabilities being a threat. Mairi, though, was keener to reclaim her unconquered Viking lineage. She hung tapestries of warrior Viking women around the kitchen, each draped in empowered sheepskin and wielding swords as they fled violence in the Outer Hebrides to settle in Icelandic lands. Those were her people, and their strength remains in her, she softly reminded Viddy one day while adjusting one of the hangings.

Just a week or so before Viddy met up with Raj and the rest, she and Mairi had a warm and hearty lunch of crab claws and buttery potatoes as the relentless grey rain chattered down like teeth on the sash-window panes. Afterwards, Mairi opened one of the kitchen drawers, the type that tax letters and batteries get thrown into, and pulled out a blue cardboard folder with *Alec Boat Photos* scrawled in black marker pen across the front. She cast out a set of rectangular prints like unorganised dominoes across the table and began sliding them around, spinning each into an angle that revealed some fragment of Alec, John, and three other boatmen fishing at sea. Bright orange rubber. Ropes. Red faces. Mairi pointed to a picture of John and Alec smiling as they each knelt over the wing of a large skate that would later be tossed back into the black depths.

—Aye, they look happy there. I bet you miss him. But I bet you also want him to leave you alone now too. You have to move on. You must.

Viddy was jarred but far from offended. Mairi was astute, dignified, and deeply perceptive enough to avoid being brash. A rare thing.

—I haven't really been looking at pictures much.

—Aye, they are a strange thing, pictures, right enough. The what-has-been. The never-will-be-again.

—It's just too hard sometimes. Too brutal.

—You'll be wanting him to leave you alone, then. I was the same with my mother. But they never leave, you know. Doesn't mean you can't, though.

Viddy's lids hung heavy as a single tear curved round her right cheek. She glanced up at the photo again. John's red-bearded beaming smile. She could hear him laugh and hated it. The meaningless of it all. No monument nor blessed public memories to keep him alive, only the weight of expectation on *her* to save him vanishing into the silent nothingness that befalls most of us who become trapped in photographic purgatory. Mairi stretched over the photographs, disordering their angled arrangement. She held Viddy's hand as tears dripped down onto the image of John and Alec, creasing their faces with damp lines. Mairi squeezed tighter.

—You've got to let him live, girl. It's the only way through.

Viddy was now sobbing.

—I want it all to go away.

—Aye, you do. But he won't. Since the body is gone, you want the rest gone too. It doesn't go. Doesn't mean you don't move on. But it doesn't go, girl. It doesn't go.

Viddy's eyes and hands and heart clasped shut then opened in one motion. She nodded as the rain chattered down heavier.

Amidst the grey light, a profusion of glittery yellow lines occasionally fell across the table, the photographs, John's face. For a split second, a vast and sandy beach spiralled out across the room and she saw them walking together.

And then it was gone.

The golden dusk was fading to dark blues and light blacks as Viddy decided where they should camp for the night. A couple of summers ago, though it seemed like years now, John showed her and the rabid twins a secret camping spot. Back then, the twins were clipped across their chests, heads shaking wildly as they set off on the path up to An Corran Beach, not far from where they were now. It was their first camping trip as a family. A golden pink sunset, the clang of steel cups, the twins tented, and a moonlit dip below twinkling stars. In the morning they walked in the footsteps of dinosaurs. Viddy hadn't been back since and, in recent months, as the summer began to present its opportunities, she continued to avoid the old spots. It was where they once were but could never be again. But today, it felt right to go back. The others lapped up her suggestion of an evening fire, tents up, lonely beach, cool wind, whisky, old souls. Even Liam was up for it.

—I'm sound tae ride, by the way.

—Are you fuck!

Raj laughed, standing over Liam, who mumbled under his breath again.

—*I doubted if I should ever come back...*

—Aye, you're not riding, Liam. No way.

Raj and Viddy turned their heads towards Bobby, who was grumbling apprehensively. He would have to take Liam's bike.

—Nae sure, like... Mind at goat? Nae sure. Och fuck it, its nae far?

Raj gently encouraged him.

—Nae far, Bobby. And yi were riding last night, fucksake!

—Aye, let's dee it!

Liam, in between poetic whispers and being hauled to his feet, protested against riding pillion, mumbling something about fucking lychee carts and goats and rampant villagers. Viddy reassured him she would ride slow. Just hang on. Tight.

Bobby, on his own firm insistence ("Nae lookin at you, lookin ahead, nae lookin back, lookin oot for masel") led the rumbling peloton out of the the Skye Mind Healers' Retreat car park. He thrust forwards, then squeezed the front brake too hard, stopping abruptly where gravel met road, bike bouncing forward, ivory horn swinging round the side of his denim jacket. He swivelled his head around slowly and profoundly, providing Raj with a nod of reassurance, frown and lips tensed in concentration as he confirmed the left turn.

—Am sound.

Raj wasn't convinced but pretended to be for his friend. He needed the confidence. Bobby jolted forwards far too quickly again, then halted suddenly, then turned, then jolted forwards some more, then turned again. They were off. They jockeyed to find themselves aligned, heading back south on the A855, Viddy tailing with a lethargic Liam slumped over, his head and helmet bouncing on her back. Since the Bluetooth headsets were linked to Liam's phone, and he was in no position to fix it, they rode on listening more attentively to the baritone rumbles of the bikes below. Liam whispered to himself over the sputtering engines, heavy breaths against the helmet microphone making it hard for the others to distinguish between breath and wind and *because it was grassy it wanted wear*. Up ahead, trundling and rumbling slowly, Bobby hit the front brake too hard again, stopping abruptly, bike leaping forwards then jamming back, only this time in he was in the middle of a road, intensely staring with great purpose into the eyes of a sheep. Viddy, concerned about the volume of crashes on invisible bends, urged him onwards. Her soft voice distorted to a crackle in the headset.

—Bobby, it happens a lot round this stretch, just rev louder and the sheep will scoot out the way!

—It's a ewe.

—So?

—Ewe, ewe, ewe... Ewe and I and a flame make three... but nae! Haha!

—What?

—Ewe to me are everything. And it's ah fine! Haha!

—Bobby...

—Ewe is my friend, not an enemy. Thank you for this exposure. This moment.

They remained static and upright in the middle of the road. Bobby locked eyes with the ewe in mutual intensity, unsure as to who or ewe or I was to look away first, lost in the moment. It felt good.

Viddy, with Liam still flopping back and forth and sideways behind her, was eager to get going. She swiftly revved past Raj and the gregarious union of man and animal, prompting the others to follow. Raj fell behind the others, dropping down into second gear to trundle along the dimming single-track road which was gently lit by the glow of his lamplight eye. The two white lines on either side of the motorcycle slowed to the pace of a cassette reel hissing towards him ambiently. In the distance, rising above the glow of two bikes and a winding road, sharp angles and peaks appeared against the darkening skyline. Raj could almost see through them, these dark glass mountains containing hours of ancestral life. Unknowable contours and passes he felt he knew but might never walk. It was the first time on the trip he began to think about his mother. Her journey, her unconditional love, and her longing. There was always longing, in everyone, one way or another. So much of Raj's youth had been spent searching for a connection with his father's life in India. A life so far removed from his own yet embedded deeply within. Leaving to visit the places he once moved in. Transporting himself back to an imagined time. Learning the cultures within. For a while, it was one way of feeling liberated from the false pretences of his supposed home and nationhood, allowing him to live under the even falser nomadic pretences of being a free-willed wanderer belonging to nowhere and nobody. Yet on the cusp of holding and harnessing and nurturing new life, it was the very idea that he did not belong anywhere in the world that became the greater oppression, the greater tyranny.

The dark glass mountains ahead elongated and stretched around, blurring Raj's vision of the road ahead. He began to experience an overwhelming series of images and thoughts bound up in the vague dusky glow. He realised how little practised he was in using his imagination to recollect other aspects of his unknowable past, at once far removed and inherent. There was a desire, even an anxiety, to let ancestors speak, lest they fall into a dark and forever silence. BUT what about his mother? He thought of her again. Perhaps it was her unconditional love and performed rootedness that he'd taken for granted. The far removed was alluring to the imagination, and the immediate mundane. But in this moment, he realised the need to imagine again. He thought of his maternal grandmother, originally from North Uist, but forced to leave for work in Oban in the early twentieth century. Raj's mother said that granny had never stopped longing for the island. Smiles on the crossing over, tears on the way back; but his mother could never understand why. He felt her confusion.

From his grandmother's hardy, longing life in Oban came his mother. Born to the rural working class but allured by the pubs, dances, and people of Glasgow. She visited home one summer only to get her stiletto stuck in a cattle grid. Never stopped longing for "home", but never chose to live there either. And there amidst the pubs, dances, and people of Glasgow arrived Raj's father, charming and charmed, and always quick to recount the days when the langur monkeys would steal his father's mangoes in Poona.

Now here was Raj, transfixed by the undefinable dark glass mountains that might shatter at any moment. There was always longing. In everyone. Dislocation from place. Dislocation from people. Dislocation from each other. Yet in spite of this dislocation, a long and infinite chain snaked and lashed and lugged and held them all together. Feeling the chain trundle beneath his feet, Raj wondered if it was our inability to see past the few links that come before and after that troubles us most. That might explain it. Feeling the force of an unknowable greater sum. It made movement uneasy, location unclear, stillness impossible. But it was, in fact, revelatory. The glass mountains. Deptford apartments. Seaton high-rises. Himalayan hills. None of them were any more real, or any more robust, than the dark glass mountains that rose up before him, steeped in songs, ideals, and liberal sympathies that could shatter at any moment. But it didn't matter. It was okay to embrace the fragilities, inside, and outside, in all these places. A plurality of land's embrace. All part of him. All home. All longing. Harness what you can, whenever it feels right. He cranked up to third gear, and felt his chain pull him back towards the others.

Raj caught up to catch sight of Liam's unhinged head bobbing back and forth against Viddy's back. Occasionally Liam would right himself vertical, gripping the back handle of the bike and raising his chin up to meet the emerging moonlight. He watched light dance across the sky, white ribbons unfurl beneath his feet, and listened to the comforting rumbles of the road. Everything seemed familiar, like he was experiencing some kind of perpetual déjà vu in which a sense of association was attached to every single sensory experience. He was convinced everything had happened before, and perhaps it had. A never-ending dream. Pulling his head sideways towards the loch and noticing a faint reflection, he became self-aware of his fumbling, unfurling limbs and posture from a bird's eye view of the increasingly lightless landscape. It was unlike him to be out of control. Usually it would unsettle him, induce a paranoia that resulted in humour at best or violence at worst. But a strange bliss fell over his whole body and being as they moved through the limitless space, limitless time. The chains cut rhythmically through the stillness and he began to feel at ease. So often the desire to seem authentic trapped Liam in a rigid presentation of the self; a regimented task far removed from the free-spirited wanderer he often professed to be. Only in this moment it was his very inauthenticity that made him feel alive. The liberation of illness was almost like a re-wiring of consciousness. It had happened before when he had fevers with the flu or tonsilitis. A fleeting sweet spot, the calm eye between coughs and sore throats and bellyaches, where a blissful aura of peace floats in. And it didn't matter how he seemed to others – he was ill, and had no pack to lead nor pups to look after. He was ill and languid and had every right to seem fragile, and it was sheer bliss. The absence of performance. The absence of strength. Only now, that fleeting moment stretched and extended without the burden of illness, pain, cough, or cold. Liam's head bumped and tumbled off Viddy's back and he felt himself peacefully glowing in the darkening night. Everything was a performance. Reality more feigned than stage, page, or screen. He could radically transform and perform, and it could *all* be inauthentically authentic. Boy fae the schemes. Yogini. Pilates instructor. Dalmuir Diner workie. He could be anyone and everyone. Performance wasn't inauthenticity but rather the fundamental impulses that lay at the core of himself. And that was fine. It was liberating. He thought of James, Ashlene, and his mum. It would be good to walk on again at Sellick Park and smile wide-eyed about the trip. A performance. Nothing real. He thought of Raj, Viddy, and Bobby. His co-protagonists who helped him then and helped him now. This seemed all too familiar. Jesus fuck.

—*It's okay that I never existed there...*

—What was that, Liam? Can't hear you properly! Tryin to get moving a bit before dark! You okay back there?

—Shanti, Viddy. Shanti shanti.

Viddy led the way and, conscious of fading light and rising winds, pulled down on the throttle as she leaned into a turning close to the dirt track that led up to Freya's. She didn't feel like stopping now but imagined the twins all tucked up under one of her knitted blankets, probably after warm milk, homemade cookies, and forehead-kisses goodnight. Freya had been so good to them, so good to Viddy, over the past few months. She felt another pang of guilt at the purposeful distance, the cold snappy exchanges, the aloof attitude towards the community they had carved out together. Mairi reminded her last week to hold her friends close, even when they felt suffocating. Even when she wanted them gone. Viddy righted her bike to look up at the glowing road ahead, white lines spinning, chains whirring. The turn-off was soon.

They were close to An Corran Beach.

On the right path.

The past was ahead.

LEAVING GREEN SLEEVES

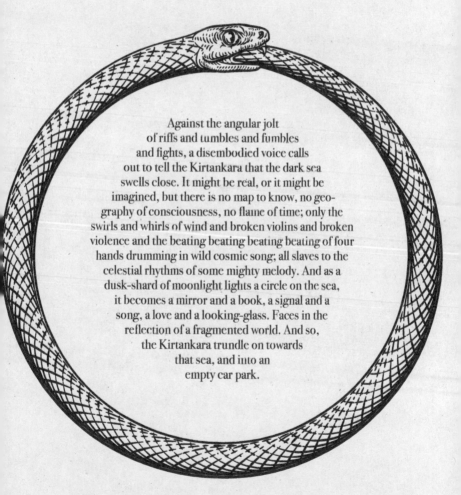

Against the angular jolt
of riffs and tumbles and fumbles
and fights, a disembodied voice calls
out to tell the Kirtankara that the dark sea
swells close. It might be real, or it might be
imagined, but there is no map to know, no geo-
graphy of consciousness, no flame of time; only the
swirls and whirls of wind and broken violins and broken
violence and the beating beating beating beating of four
hands drumming in wild cosmic song; all slaves to the
celestial rhythms of some mighty melody. And as a
dusk-shard of moonlight lights a circle on the sea,
it becomes a mirror and a book, a signal and a
song, a love and a looking-glass. Faces in the
reflection of a fragmented world. And so,
the Kirtankara trundle on towards
that sea, and into an
empty car park.

○

Bobby left his harmonium strapped to the bike, opting to help with the tents and Tennent's, which he packed into the hemp sack and slung over his shoulder. They scuttled along a path of sand and soil and seagrass. Dusk grew darker and the land began to merge with the clouds overhead. The narrow path widened to form a mossy square patch overlooking the greys and blacks of sand below, waves gently lapping in, and a silhouette of Staffin Island in the distance. This was the camping spot. The ashes of an old fire remained. An imperfect etching on the land, slowly becoming greener with moss, burn marks barely visible. Viddy couldn't remember if it was the exact same fire she and John had stood by. Perhaps not. Perhaps it didn't matter if she imagined it to be. It was nice to be there. Nice to imagine. Nice to remember again.

Below the heavy clouds and overhanging cliffs, black cattle ambled on and around the ashy sands which inked into green fields on one side and dark seas on the other. Ragged seaweed swirled in patches. Bobby broke the silence that seemed to have pacified them in that place and moment, prompting the unpacking of tents.

—Sea cows. Tents up, aye?

Liam rolled to one side, unfurling a sleeping bag which he curled into while the others extended poles, danced in the wind with rattling tarps, and foraged for firewood in the grey and blue and turquoise light. Liam seemed to be at peace simply watching, listening, embracing the soporific serenity of seeing people just be. Viddy carefully placed rocks around the etching, old ashes gently blowing to dust, and arranged a new pile of twigs. A pyre.

After an extended period of concentration and indecision, Bobby decided to leave the paraffin lamp in his hemp sack, carefully tucking it into a tarp corner of Great-Granda Duthie's flapping Dunkirk tent. Instead, he reached into his inside dungaree pocket for a packet of Scottish Bluebell matches he saved for special occasions. The matchbox sandpaper was offset by a delicate watercolour print of bluebells against the green and purple rolling hills that he knew were never wild but remained special nonetheless. Years ago, as a young loon, he would read football trivia from the back of these matchboxes to Granda Duthie. Granda Duthie knew most of the answers already, but Bobby enjoyed acting out the ceremony no less. This specific matchbox, bought in an antique shop up the West End, read, *Which winger played for Celtic and Scotland before World War Two, and for Manchester United and Scotland after it?* Bobby had memorised the answer. Jim Delaney. Scottish Bluebells. His very own madeleines. He later found out that the same match company marketed the very same product as ENGLAND'S GLORY south of the border, replete with two Union Jacks and an image of an HMS battleship. Imperial glory for English fires; purple heather for the romantic barbarians above. If the taste for matches (the match market?) was so devolved back then, then wouldn't that mean... Bobby felt Viddy place a hand on his shoulder, as he caught focus of the darkening sea he'd been staring at but not seeing.

—You alright, Bobby? You did well on the bike back there.

—Aye, cheers. Sorry about the ewe.

— Looked like you had a good chat, no worries. D'yi want to spark up the fire? I'll get the cans and food sorted.

—Aye. Got matches here. Where's Raj?

—Getting more firewood. Should be sorted for the night.

With the poise and delicacy of an overweight gymnast, Bobby sprung up and carefully selected a single match. In one precise strike against the pungent sandpaper strip, he cupped a flame which crackled the first bits of bark and newspaper that Viddy had placed before him. Liam watched on, gentle smile fixed upon an already transfixed face. Bobby blew gently under the glow, flames rising, flapping, crackling, wavering in the wind. Raj arrived cradling more driftwood to burn, and Viddy completed the circle, cans in hand, bottle in bag. It felt good to watch the flames burn to nothing. Liam whispered something again.

—*To where it bent in the undergrowth. It's okay that I never existed there...*

After a few minutes of flame crackle and warmth, a gentle darkness descended upon the imperfect circle they had formed around the fire. The ambience was peaceful. Liam had roused to a livelier state, and Raj reflected on the strange beauty of conversation around a fire at dark; the irony of being anywhere and nowhere and somewhere, yet needing to be somewhere to be nowhere. Staffin ahead, Skye behind, all in mind, not in sight. The sound of lapping waves was maybe just wind, the ashy grey beach had turned black, but, nevertheless, they imagined it was there. Bobby reached into his hemp sack for the speaker.

He'd forgotten about the playlist he created a few days ago, asking the others to add a few songs each via text message. It was democratic. He thumbed his phone, pressed shuffle, and sparked a rollie in anticipation. Snares. Tambourines. Walking bass. Tanging riff. Freda Payne's "Band of Gold". His choice. Spirits rising. Balvenie pouring. Smiles across the fire.

—Absolute tune. D'ya ken there's a SITAR solo in that song?! A SITAR solo in a soul song! I mean, fit the...

Bobby turned the volume up, catching himself unable to fully articulate amidst excitement. Bobby very rarely raised his voice or altered its intonation, but when he did, it cranked the energy levels of those around him like some stoic farmer's trump trading card. Raj shouted back across, through flames, over Freda's lament.

—Bit out of place here!

—How? Tune's a tune.

—Aye, it's a tune.

Laughter reverberated around them. Viddy threw her hair, neck, and shoulders back and forth. Liam, a surprisingly camp and rhythmic mover, roused himself to snare-nod and shoulder-shud his way through the song. Raj nodded along, smiling, and looking down at his wedding ring aglow with the reflective orange flames. The sitar solo chimed, Freda stepping back. Raj thought of Ibti, of unconditional love, of family, all within the passing, refracting flames of a second. He shouted back, straining to hear himself.

—Aye, it's a tune but it's just not true. It can't just be a band of gold that's left. What about the memories? They never leave.

—Aye, but that's exactly phit she says! It's *remembering* what love was. And the dreams, ken.

—Aye, okay.

The song, typical of those Holland-Dozier-Holland Motown hits, began to gradually fade without changing melody. Just quieter and quieter until such time it would play again. Bobby was quick to quip with more context. Apparently, he was on first-name terms now.

—Aye, Freda was actually older sister to Scherrie, of Diana Ross and The Supremes fame. But yi can see that Freda was the Solange to Scherrie's Beyoncé. Ah, that style, independence, sass, artistic flair. Ah void of pop marketing, ana! And me, phit a beautiful woman she wiz ana...

Bobby's voice faded as the deeply twanging introduction to the next song pulsed out of the tinny speakers and into the night. Tammy Wynette's "Stand By Your Man".

—Phit?! Phasizat?

Viddy, unsheepishly, raised her hand, smiling, to Raj's quiet surprise.

—Mine. I love this song.

—Really, Viddy?

—Why not?

—Well, the tune's cool, love that wobbling electric. But this woman. This woman, Vid! Her man out beatin and cheatin, and she's just like, aye, that's cool, come home for a hug. I love you anyway.

—Bullshit!

—How?

—Hear how fucking derisory she's being? He's *just a man*. And yet she still can't escape a society that demands she has to stand by this bonehead.

—Thought it was an anti-feminist anthem?

—Think she could control that shit? It's like chick-lit love for Jane Austen. People not realising she's actually ripping the piss out of the past her fans seemingly aspire to be in...

—You've thought about this a lot!

—I just love that line, he's *just a man*. I guess a part of her still needs him too.

—Aye, but what did she actually mean? Like, personally? Was she a feminist?

—Fuck does that matter?

Viddy's unintended mic-drop moment faded as Tammy's poignant last rasp filled the black island air. Liam and Bobby watched the exchange, smiling at the fond friction of the past. They hadn't seen Viddy and Raj speak to each other with that glint since, well, older times, different skins. And they kept going. The beautiful mundane purity of speaking shite in the dark island night. Music on, drinks flowing, vowels burring, hearts purring.

—Mon, Viddy. Yi can do better than fuckin Tammy Wynette!

—Alright, alright. Fuckin fascist, man. Pass the phone here. Got something new to shut yer wee face up. It's a band called Big Thief.

—That's the shit, Viddy. Knew yi could do better.

—Fuck you, man. Tammy is sound!

A low grumbling crunch bellowed out above them, before a fragile voice rose up and swirled with the smoke puffing out from dying embers. The voice whispered about energies reeling, clouds in space, lines on faces, long black hair, winning, spinning, and planets. It broke into a distorted cry that celebrated the hopelessness of altering anything that was already written.

Like four Shaivites entranced, the Kirtankara nodded along in time. Or beyond time.

Was this ritual? Ceremony? That rare feeling of being in the right place with the right people? Again? Not without mishap. Not without happenstance. Not without luck and love and memory and persistence. Liam was beaming, looking at Raj.

—It's mad, but. How we can aw listen to the same tune, but hear it differently, y'know?

—Jesus Christ, man. What?

—Naw, seriously. I remember ma papi's funeral. Cunt wanted "You'll Never Walk Alone" belt oot as he got carted intate the fire! Anyways. Ah wiz smiling. So happy, man. Thinking o him and me at Sellick Park. But looks over to ma maw and she wiz greetin bad. Mental, man. Same song had us happy and sad in the same moment. Nae uniformity. Jist these textures of emotion. It was oor differences that made us whole again, y'kno?

—That no an Atomic Kitten song?

—Aye. Stick them oan!

—But, aye, think I see what you mean. Like, it's not the subjective experience of one of us that matters. It's the collective. The shared sense of ceremony. I guess the shared sense of ceremony in death.

Swirling, curling, and quivering guitar lines bleat out in the black night, before a high-pitched buzz of feedback brought the song to its death. Then silence, and Liam's voice as he turned to Raj.

—Fucks knows, man. Mad.

—Anyway. Your turn – what's it ti be?

—Fuck, man. Cannae follow youz! Just pass the phone here, will yi...

A baritone rasped about the promises of dawn. And mornings after.

—This takes me back, man. Or mibbe forwards. Mibbe the past is always in front of us. Like, yi always have to go back to *imagine* the future, otherwise it cannae happen.

—Fuck knows, man. It's been a long day. Need some kip. We all do.

And with great ceremony the album ushered them into a deep sleep as the flames died down in the blackness of the island night, unfolding, as everything does, into ash, dust, particles, memories, moons, and meteorites.

THE

EPILOGUE

A ROADSIDE SOUTH OF STAFFIN

The four of them sat eating sugary pocket-sized shortbread on a roadside somewhere south of Staffin. Liam thumbed through his phone to find a song for the road ahead. They slipped on their helmets. It was Pink Floyd's 'Time'. They were older, nearer to death. But there was still time to kill before that.

Liam looked skywards, Bobby rode Nicholson one last time, Raj braced himself for births to come.

Stretching out her back, Viddy looked across to Staffin Island.

And the birds sang, and the seagrass danced, and she knew he wasn't dead at all. None of them were.

The past was just ahead of them.

One day, this would be written.

ABOUT THE AUTHOR

Arun Sood is a Scottish-Indian writer, musician and academic working across multiple forms. He was born in Aberdeen to a West-Highland Mother and Punjabi father, and has since lived in Glasgow, Amsterdam, DC, and now Plymouth, South Devon. Arun's critical and creative practice ranges from academic publications, editorials, poetry and fiction to ambient musical tapestries. Broadly, his varied outputs engage with diasporic identities, mixed-race heritage, ancestry, language and memory.